THE NEVERBORN

A Young Adult Dystopian Novel

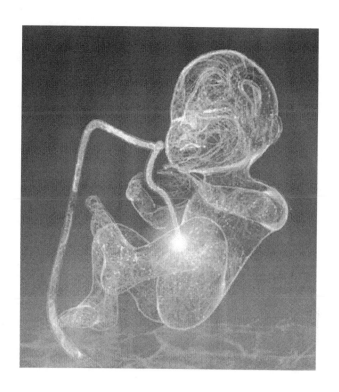

B.B. BRIGHTON

THE NEVERBORN

CHAPTER ONE

Kekoa

October 2048

My love of adventure jangles all my senses as we bounce up the scant trail into the jungle—towners don't get to do this. I hang onto Dad's waist with one hand; the other grips the sensorbrace on the back of his motorcycle. My jaw clatters from the bumpy cane trail, but every clump of Guinea grass we pass brings me closer to our pig hunt. I hear the high-pitched squeals of the panicked boar and see their wild eyes in my mind. My legs tense. We might die if a pig gored us; fortunately, my "brothers", Canyon and Kana, and I are excellent shots. Not only do pigs destroy the land, and root up people's yards and gardens, but they also spread plant disease killing Ohia trees. The devils.

My heart accelerates its drumbeat the closer we draw to the start. We rumble up the ancient cane trail, and I punch my fist into the air and whoop. Kana and Canyon do the same piggybacked on their rig behind us. Even our golden Labrador, Mischief, in the sidecar beside me, barks. She reminds me of the dog grinning on the book cover of *Old Yeller*, which Dad read to me as a kid. The Kauai mountain ridge's claw-carved cliffs above call me to this wild country in Hawaii.

I lean my forehead into the back of Dad's t-shirt to keep from getting cut by the tiny razors on each of the blades of ten-foot-tall guinea grass hanging over the trail. A few stalks blow over us and brush against my left arm and ear. My arm itches, but I can't scratch it now. We jostle on our motorcycle, maneuvering around rocks. Finally, we reach the forest of albizia trees covering a ravine in front of us. I'll be glad to cool off in the shade. It's already 80 degrees, and it's only nine in the morning.

Bending over the sidecar, I get our gear and buckle on my knife and sheath. Mischief prances in excitement and wants to lick my face. "No, girl." I push her sixty-pound golden body to the side. I take out knives in their leather belts to hand my brothers, while Kana pulls the arrows and compound crossbows out of the other sidecar. He sets mine next to the cycle. It's hard not to talk above a whisper, but we understand to stay quiet. The adrenaline pumping through me is anything but quiet.

I hand Canyon his belt. Without taking it, he staggers back, clutching his stomach. "You got me, my brother, my friend. I'd die for you, and you—you—"

There's glee in his eyes. He backs up and falls. Golden hair spreads over the green grass. Eyes the color of faded blue jeans open, still as a rock. Okay, movie star wannabe, I'll play your game.

I grab the canvas bag we'll later fill with a pig carcass, cover him, and whisper, "As long as you're dead, *you* can be our pig bait. Who needs a burial anyway?"

He springs to life and starts chasing me with the bag, so I leap down the gully, laughing through my nose. One leg stretches in front and hopes for a soft landing. I slip on ferns and roll into the crumbling fronds.

Canyon hikes down the gully and spreads our bait of overripe papaya and guava plum under a tree. He looks at me, and a Cheshire grin spreads across his face. "Here's Kekoa's sweet curly head, and here's his little brown butt. Here piggy, piggy." He whispers.

I chuckle, signal to Kana to grab my crossbow, and trudge up the underbrush to the other side. *But it's Canyon's blond, shiny hair, and Herculean muscles the girls at the market talk about.* I shove the thought aside and wish it wouldn't keep coming back.

Poor Kana. His name means "love" in Japanese, which he is, but he can't even look at a girl. Kana picks his way down the ravine and shakes his head at our mirthful stupidity. He gives me my weapon and cuts a few plate-size Philodendron leaves that wind around a nearby albizia tree. Kana slices them, so they fold into each other and form a mat for a place to sit—neat freak that he is.

Dad's rig rumbles up the ridge with Mischief away from us. She's good at flushing pigs down toward the fruit. Canyon, Kana, and I whistle the mynah bird squawk and wave our arms so we can identify each other's locations and space ourselves. Kana stays closest to the motorcycles. Canyon takes the middle of the gully, and I head to the far side about twenty-five yards from the fruit. My shirt smells like a compost pile after the roll in the ferns, but I don't care. We've had pigs bolt toward us, but the wily animals haven't hurt us—yet.

I lick my finger and hold it up to see which direction the wind is blowing. The pigs will come down the ravine from the mountains. I pick a spot behind a rock where I don't think the swine will detect my scent, even when they reach the fruit. Sweat trickles down my back, and I taste salt on my lips. We have to hit the exact spot at the base of the sow's necks to kill them immediately. Otherwise, they'll run a mile with our hundred-dollar arrows hanging out of their bodies. Plus, they'll suffer. Our orange bait shows amid the green underworld. I'm ready.

Canyon plays an ancient Gameboy that Dad bought online, barely visible through the shrubs and ginger plants. Kana immerses himself in a newspaper he found in the trash at the market.

A tickle on my leg makes me jump. I scout for centipedes, but it's an ant. Kicking over a rock makes a fifteen-inch centipede crawl out. If only I'd brought the machete to cut the long curmudgeon into crumbs. Better to squat among the ferns than sit and have one crawl up my shorts.

Mischief barks up the mountain. She'll be on a leash, so the pigs won't kill her with their powerful tusks and rip her body apart with their ferocious teeth. Dad said pigs are smarter than dogs, and they can chew up a human in minutes, bones and all. In seconds, they could annihilate Mischief. Some of my steam settles at that thought. *God, keep her safe.*

Soon, we hear snorting and the padding of feet. The young adult swine meander down first, followed by females. A black sow and her ten piglets are closest to me. The males come last, highest on the pecking order. They have longer hair sticking up on their shoulders and heads. They smell sweet and musky, like body odor. We wait for them to discover the fruit, and Canyon whistles the shama thrush song to signal. It's time to shoot. We all descend from our perches and aim our bows at the tastier female pigs. My shot pierces just above the shoulder blades of a black one with brown spots. A perfect shot. She drops dead. Other pigs look from side to side, wild-eyed. Another falls on Kana's side.

The swine return to chomping on the papaya. Canyon's shot hits the shoulder of a dark brown sow. She turns, squeals her outrage, and her eyes deadlock on Canyon. He steps forward, fumbling to put another arrow in his bow. None of us can land a shot at the base of her neck that will kill her now because she's turned. Too close. The sow stomps. She lowers her tusks and charges him. He drops his crossbow and runs up the mountain.

"Whoa, baby," he yells. Something catches his foot. He trips and falls.

I drop my bow and leap down the ravine, dodging shrubs between me and the beast. "Go. Out. Go!"

The hundred-fifty-pound sow stops and looks at me, snorts a summons, and runs toward my brother. Her gouging tusks lower. Too close. Canyon pushes himself up to run, but it's too late. He's going to get gored.

I leap on her back, reaching to pull forward her front leg the way we've practiced on tuskless pigs. She falls. I twist her head back and scramble to kneel at her nose. Her legs are flying as she tries to stand, but my headlock keeps her from gaining traction. Her enraged squeal screams through the forest, frenzied. She's ready to rip me apart. Still holding her head down, I pull out my knife with my right hand and slit her throat before she can jump up. I don't know if I got deep enough. I jump back, holding my hands out, ready to fight knife against tusks. She kicks to the side and stands. The forest vibrates from her shriek. Her eyes show murder. But too much of her blood is gone, and she sinks back to the ground. Huffing her contempt, she drops—dead.

Canyon brushes himself off and yells at the pigs who have meandered back, "Go, you stupid idiots! Go. Go." The herd scampers down the gully. "What's up with you? I would have gotten away." Canyon stares at me.

I throw my knife down. "You could have been gored and bled to death right here. It's not like we have health insurance. Have you noticed that none of our parents ever take us to a hospital? Not that we could get there in time from here, anyway." As I speak, my body is one giant beating heart. Trembling zigzags through me.

Dad rides the rig down the cane path above us and stops. I run up through the ferns and underbrush to bury my head in Mischief's silky fur. What if the sow had gored Canyon? I don't even want to tell Dad. My frustration makes me want to scratch valleys in the mountains with my own hands. Mischief licks my face, still tied inside Dad's sidecar. I hug her and relax.

"Come on. Help us string up this bacon," Canyon yells from below.

I bolt down. Dad follows me to the carcasses.

"Good job, boys. You got three?"

"Yeah, Kekoa tackled the big sow. She started chasing me," Canyon says. He looks at me and hands me my knife. His eyes say, *don't tell your dad.* "Too bad we can't sign up for football on Kauai. Kekoa would be a star tackle." Canyon scours the area to find his crossbow.

"Yeah, and you could be a star, flirting with the girls in the stands." The resentment in my voice surprises me.

"Don't I wish." Canyon laughs.

Dad swallows hard. "If only we lived in a world where you could play football and flirt with girls like everyone else."

He thinks it's fine to flirt? I'm surprised. Dad seems uncomfortable whenever Canyon spends too much time talking to girls at the market.

Kana and Canyon go from pig to pig, slitting their throats. I find a strong tree limb within reach and throw three ropes over it. We gut them and hang the carcasses by their back feet to bleed out.

Canyon eyes me as if he doesn't know what to make of my previous burst of anger. After the last pig hangs, he says, "Thanks, Bro. I love you too." His hands are on his hips. With his rippling muscles and blood splatter, he looks like the star of some testosterone-filled movie where ninety percent of the film is fighting. I love him. And right now, I hate him.

I thump his shoulder with my fist. *You have no idea. Life is a game to you.*

Kana uses a water bottle to clean his arms and hands, wiping them off with leaves. He turns to Dad, "But why? Uncle, why do we have to live isolated in our canyon and only come to Lihue on market days to sell and hunt?"

Dad's shoulders slump. His mouth tightens, and his eyebrows lower like a bowed branch. "I can't tell you. Not yet."

"Come on." Canyon sounds like he can conquer the world in a single attack. "We've all finished our high school online programs. It's not like we don't understand politics. You've taught us all about world history and current events.

Why can't you tell us why we have to grow up isolated? Is it viruses?"

"No. The news always hypes current events into garnering more supporters. As pathogens mutate, they become weaker. We want to expose you to various viruses to build your immunity. That's part of the reason we go to Lihue every week and sell produce." Dad sighs and looks at Canyon and Kana. "Your folks, and my wife and I, love you all so much. You've been all raised together and call me Uncle, but you're all like my sons. You realize that, right?" His eyes stroke each cheek, including mine, with his love. I think he's remembering when we were babies, then toddlers, and children. Now we're almost men, tall, strong, and smart. He's poured his vast knowledge into us all.

We become stone sober. Every inch of our hearts longs to know why. Why do other kids have young parents? Usually single moms. We have three older married couples, and three boys all the same age, one for each couple. And no one will tell us why they've kept us away from the public eye.

I put my hand on my father's shoulder. "Please, Dad. We're not children anymore."

Dad leans into my touch and shakes his head. He looks like he could cry.

Kana pulls the newspaper out from the folded package he'd tucked into the back of his pants. "Uncle, The Guardian reports about an abortionist's arrest. She's facing kidnapping charges if they can prove she delivered live babies seventeen years ago. The birth mothers didn't know or give consent." He hands Dad the paper.

Dad brushes the crumbly rocks from an outcropping and eases his arthritic hips onto the forest floor and reads the article. Glancing up at me, he pats the ground next to him, inviting me to sit. Dad bites the side of his lower lip as if the fangs inside him are eating him away from the inside out. "It's time." His lips twist. He turns his skinny Santa-gray head to stare at us all. "Sit down. I'll tell you."

Canyon plops on a rock, and Kana sits on his mat. I nestle next to my dad. All is quiet. Even the birds stop singing.

"Seventeen years ago, an OBGYN doctor didn't want to refer patients for abortions, even though the government required her to do so. So, she became an abortionist specializing in late-term pregnancies." His tone carries the importance of the world.

I exhale, shake my head, and notice the pig blood on my hands. "Whoa," I say. Pictures in videos Dad showed us hang in my head. He had us debate both sides of the abortion issue with each other. What did the abortionist see? Which type of procedure did she prefer? The pictures in my head make me want to cry. I can't imagine why he's telling us this, or what it has to do with us.

Dad puts up his hand. "Only Dr. Lavada didn't abort the babies. She had a clinic built so she could deliver the infants, clamp, and cut the umbilical cords instantly. Then she pushed them through a drawer in the wall before they cried while the drugged birthmothers listened to music in their headphones. A nurse on the other side of the wall had incubators to care for each child. The birthmothers saw a bowl of afterbirth being carried out and thought the babies were dead, but they weren't. There were fewer complications, too. Dr. Lavada's ratings were high, and no one died. At our church, someone found families to take the babies." He pauses. His eyes search us one by one. "Each of you is one of those rescued by Dr. Lavada."

"What?" I ask.

I see Canyon's head jut forward. His eyes bug out.

Kana's mouth is partway open.

I realize mine is too.

My mind plays back to Dad's words — "Each of you is one of "those" rescued."

Those throwaway babies whose mothers didn't want them.

I stare at Kana and Canyon's lost eyes.

Lost.

Like a chick when a hen moves on without it, cheeping for hours until it dies under the blistering sun. Lost. Like the baby left to die amid crashing waves on a remote Kapaa beach, wailing for hours, until it doesn't. Lost. Like the hiker who takes a wrong turn, can't find his way out, and dies of dehydration. Lost.

I'm aware of a dramatic shift inside me. In my sense of who I am, I'm one of "those" babies. Something inside me, under me, through me is gone.

Kana's voice is as soft as a downy feather but bathed in sadness. "I always thought we were your grandchildren. Mom said we were adopted. I guess it doesn't make sense. I appear Japanese. Kekoa looks Hawaiian, and only Canyon is Caucasian with his blond hair. I wanted to believe we were your grandchildren. But are any of us related to you or our mothers and fathers?"

"No." Dad's eyes are watery. Each word seems to come out as if saying it cuts him with a knife. "Each of you came from Dr. Lavada's clinic. We all lived in or around Lihue. When we heard about this opportunity, we prayed about it and pooled our resources to raise you together. We leased our canyon from the Spragues and spent a year getting it ready while you were babies. No one could know about you."

"Why not?" Canyon's voice has the desperation of a starved kitten. "Why are we a secret?"

Dad looks down and brushes off his pants as if having clean ones will give him more strength to answer the question. He holds up the newspaper. "Because what Dr. Lavada did was illegal."

"But she saved our lives. What can be illegal about that?" I pick a fern up next to me and rub it between my fingers. My understanding of morality has just been smashed. How can people twist right and wrong? An ache throbs deep within. I wish I could climb up a ridge of our canyon and think about this under the puffy clouds.

"It's illegal if the government passes laws that say so," Kana says. "Just because a country makes a law doesn't make it right. I remember you teaching us that in our civics classes." He clears his throat and swallows a thousand tears. "We can never leave our canyon or let anyone realize we're alive."

He's seeing the implications before I can even wrap my head around each of us, resulting from a failed abortion.

"It's more complicated than merely being at risk. The police arrested Dr. Lavada last week." Dad chokes up. The paper drops from his hand. I pick it up for him. "They accused her of kidnapping, as if," he blinks, and a wash of pain covers his face. "We heard the police will refer kids without identity chips to the Army." His hands cover his cheek as if he can't believe he said it.

I stand. "But we don't have chips."

"Exactly," Dad says and steadies himself to stand. He puts his hand on my shoulder.

Chips with social security numbers get embedded at birth. They give you financial status, and the ability to buy, sell, get paid, and pay taxes.

He sighs. "In the government's eyes, you are Neverborns."

"The police hunt down Neverborns because our mothers didn't want their children?" Canyon stands.

Dad grimaces and rubs his hip. His wrinkles reflect the time he's given us out of his previously normal life. "They aren't looking specifically for you. Right now, they're hunting down the adults who took the babies." He chuckles. "Like me. If they find you, they'll induct you into the military and funnel you off to the war in Thailand. But they won't prosecute you. They'll give your lives, and probably your deaths, to the military."

Canyon swears, and Dad doesn't rebuke him. The breeze ruffles the leaves as if life is normal. As if we could go back to our private, carefree canyon. As if we can ride on our kayaks and our zipline, surf, swim, sing together every night, play board games, take our classes, and share our happy lives.

The swine guts lie close to the tree, smelling like a mix of blood and bile. The odor makes me nauseous. My guts seem to be among the pigs.

The swine will be back after we leave and eat up all the blood and guts. Ironic. They'll eat their own. Like our government, which takes innocent kids and pours them into their military stomachs.

CHAPTER TWO

Kekoa

"Show off." Canyon says and ribs me, but I see the shredding of his heart in his eyes.

I shake my head and help Canyon and Kana pack the bagged carcasses into the sidecars, and we ride up to Sprague's ranch. Dad takes the sow's ears in a plastic sack up the stairs to the Koa wood front door and returns with money while we all wash under their outdoor showerhead on the side of their huge plantation-style brown house. We resemble zombies as we take off our bloody pants and shirts to stash and put on our clean clothes from the rainbow cloth tote. I glance at the sun. It must be about two in the afternoon. My stomach rumbles, but I don't want to think about food. My heart has fallen into a crevasse, alone and unwanted.

Once we've loaded the pig meat onto our cycles, we crawl down the old sugarcane roads. It's about eighty-two degrees. The sky is almost cloudless. Breezes whistle over me. *Lord, thank You for the pig meat and for keeping us all safe, but what future can we have now?*

I hug Dad with both arms, riding on the back of the motorcycle. If only I could keep him forever. My very life puts him in danger. We come to the smooth roads of the highway. I think about my parents and Canyon and Kana's parents—my two aunties, two uncles. Not just family, but the people who gave up their homes, first children, and grandchildren to raise us. To give us lives. When the world saw tissue in a bucket, they saw children.

When we arrive, Dad and I put the meat into the van and pack it with ice. His eyes are red. I can't look at him or I'll cry. The cooler holds sandwiches and water. I drag it behind the tent and sit on it to eat, watching people drift by. My peanut butter and pineapple jelly sandwich stare at me from my lap, untouched. Shoppers' eyes flit about. Most locals have brown eyes—like mine. I wonder if I'm related to them.

The flowers and bananas on our stand have sold. Still, the avocado and vegetables are available for sale. I scan the area for girls but decide we need a "brother" powwow.

"Kana, Canyon, yo."

They stand next to me, eating their sandwiches.

"The thing is, our lives put our parents in danger," I say.

"Yeah, it sucks. But what can we do about it?" Canyon fans his hand out.

"I don't know. We have to leave and go somewhere," I say.

"Where can we go when we can't work without a social security number? We were never born, remember?" Venom emanates from Canyon. "I'm not joining the military."

"I want to attend college. Live on campus," I say with my hands on my hips and think about sitting in class with girls on either side.

"Me too," Kana nods. "Think about it. Our mothers wanted us dead. Dead. Our futures are dead without their approval. What's that?"

Canyon balls a fist and walks off, arms stiff as a stick. His face is vermilion red. We're gutted, all of us—like our pigs. He kicks at a nearby chicken who squawks and flies off.

Kana watches him go, a tear trickling down his face. He wipes his eyes with the gray surfer logo t-shirt he's wearing and walks off.

I gaze at Dad. *Lord, protect my family.*

Dad's news has just blown out all the support beams that kept my heart afloat. Seeing my brothers in the same gutter makes it three times worse. I find Dad to tell him I'm going to the bathroom and walk toward the tan outhouse across the field. Mom takes money from a customer with three more ladies in line at the stand. I long to hug her, feel her soft hand pressing my head against her shoulder, and smell the lavender cream she uses on her face and neck.

Visualizations fill my mind with the births I've seen in the movies. They have happy parents shedding tears of joy. But no tears of joy came when I slid out. Only relief. It was done. I was done. As if my beating heart had less value than a rock thrown into the ocean. My chest hurts. *"God, please don't let Mom and Dad go to prison. It was me who was supposed to die, not them."* I kick the grass. My gut feels like seaweed swishing in the ocean currents.

A twenty-something-year-old man ambles over to me. He's my height with the pasty white face of someone who spends all his time inside glued to media. He has a nasty sore under his chin next to a gold necklace with a word centered starting with "B-l-a." I can't see the rest because his shirt is covering it. It must be his name or the name of his girlfriend. A flashing gadget illumines from in his hand, something I've never seen before. He smiles and turns it off.

"Hey, my name is Clint. You live here? Does your family do this?" His hand gestures out toward the stands of growers on both sides of us. His dark slicked back hair appears as if glue holds it in place. The amber earring shaped like a golden eye coordinates with the eagle tattoo on his ear.

"Yeah. We live somewhat close. This is how we make our living." I stare at his earring.

"Listen." He laughs, but something seems off as if he's laughing because he doesn't want to talk to me. "I work on the ship in the harbor, the *Golden Princess*. Have you ever thought about working on a cruise ship?" He curls his fingers in and out, a nervous habit perhaps, but the tone of his voice is rich and smooth. His eyes scan the market and then come back to me.

Work on a cruise ship? Yesterday? Perhaps, when I didn't know who I am. Today? No way. Not without a chip. But I can't tell him that. He might turn me in to the authorities. My parents would go to jail. Kana, Canyon, and I would end up in a military camp on the front lines in the proxy war in Thailand. But this could be my way out. If I disappeared, my folks would be safe. "Do they require experience?"

"No," he says. His eyes assess my frame. "You're strong. Are you at least seventeen?"

"Yes." I stammer, "What kind of paperwork do you need to work on the ship?"

"That's the thing." He moves closer and whispers. "You don't need any. Take my place with my badge, my chip, my identity. You become me. I heard on the news about the brave parents who stepped up to raise abandoned babies. I know." His eyes drill a tunnel into my brain.

My heart pummels my chest. I step back. He knows. Maybe this is God's answer to my prayer to protect my family. How do I know? Is the chip the mark of the beast? Will it get turned into a way to persecute Christians? But not having it persecutes people now.

"And you. What would you do?" I pretend to cough to cover for my reedy voice.

"I'd be free to roam your beautiful island." He gestures out with both hands. Clint speaks with an East Coast accent.

"But you wouldn't have any status. You couldn't buy or sell. You'd be no one," I say.

He laughs that fake laugh again and tilts his head. "You're so concerned about me. That's touching." He pauses. "Don't be. I have friends who will take care of me." He puts his palms up. "Do you want to sail the seas and explore the world? My little gadget is a social security number reader. It shows that you don't have one. This is your chance."

I look across the field at my father and mother.

A buckshot pang hits my gut. I squeeze my thumbs in my hands and break out in a sweat. The world tunnels. *If I don't, will he turn us in?*

"Yes." I blink back tears.

CHAPTER THREE

Silver

The head of security, Silver, leans back in his chrome office chair on the Golden Princess cruise ship, reaching his hands behind his head and arching back to stretch. Cool air shushes from its white woven fabric. Ten computer screens form a half-circle around him and show normal activity for docking time at Port Nawiliwili, on Kauai. His phone vibrates, and he picks it up. It's Blake.

"Yeah?" Silver scratches his orange and white beard.

"You were right. I found one. Easy as picking up a baby out of a crib. Innocent as a lamb. He believed every lie I told him, including telling him that I am Clint." He laughs. "And he believed it all."

Blake's voice sounds elated. *It's about time the loser does something right.* "Keep talking." Silver picks up a toothpick, rocks in his chair, and works over the food trapped between his molars.

"A news article came out last week. Seems an abortionist delivered babies for seventeen years and then moved. You said…" Blake scratches the back of his head.

Silver puts down the toothpick. "I read the article. Tell me about your catch." "Idiot," slips from his mouth quietly.

"Like you said, teens are at the farmer's market who don't have chips. Three boys. I talked to one, Kekoa. He said he'd do it. The guy turned white when I told him I knew as if I had caught him." Blake cackles with a hiccup-sound.

Silver blows a raspberry sound away from the phone and shakes his head. *What I have to put up with. But I don't want to discourage Blake now.* "What a stupid name. Does he think he's a tree?"

Blake goes silent for a second and then says, "No. The name Kekoa is Hawaiian. It means brave warrior. It's k e k o, a, but the letter 'e' is pronounced as an 'a' in the Hawaiian language."

Silver feels heat creeping up his neck. "I know that. What does he look like? I'll alert security."

"Oh, he's about six-foot tall, thin. Dark-skinned, maybe a mix of races like most Hawaiians. He's nice."

Silver chuckles. "Nice and naïve. Okay. When should we expect him?" Silver waits as the sound of Blake gulping a drink of water comes over the line. "Blake. When?"

"I left him five minutes ago. He's walking the three miles to the port, so an hour or two."

"Whose chip did you put in him?" Silver picks up his toothpick again. This is going well.

"Clint's. He's a drug addict I chippered and then dumped in the forest. I told Kekoa I was Clint and needed someone to take my place on the ship." His voice echoes pride.

A little bravado is okay as long as Blake remembers who's boss. Silver nods his head. One side of his mouth rises in a slight grin. "And he bought it?"

Blake laughs. "Oh, yeah. I even gave him 'my' uniform."

"Did you tell him to check in with Troy in housekeeping and give him his room number?"

"Of course. I'm not dumb."

"What did you do with the real Clint?"

Blake snorts and chuckles. "He was higher than a kite in his tent when I chloroformed him. I took his chip, then ditched him off a cliff in the mountains. The pigs will pack away his skinny carcass in no time."

"Any witnesses?"

Blake swears. "No. It was dark, man. He wasn't even a part of the homeless community. I talked to him for a while before he shot up. He'd flown from LA to escape his parents and do drugs. I cleaned out his bank account before I gave Kekoa his chip. He had over seven grand. Joint account with daddy." He snickers.

"Remember, I get half. Don't mess with me." Silver picks up the tabletop picture of his young daughter. They have the same eyes. Her sweet red curls wind around her fair skin and angel-kiss freckles. She'll be short, like him. Cool for a girl, not a boy. Teasing, getting beat up, people not taking you seriously, girls not wanting you—happen because you're short. Thanks a lot, God. Well, money has a way of changing all that.

"Partners. I'll put your share where you told me, in the Panama account." Blake sniffs.

He better not be doing meth again. Silver puts the picture down. "You got extra DNA from the body to give me, so we can frame the new 'Clint'?" I can kill him anytime without repercussion once I've planted evidence to cover myself. He's a Neverborn. No one can trace anything to me.

Blake swears again. "You never told me. Now, I'll have to go back. It'll take hours to hike down the ravine and find the slimy carcass. And there may not be much left." He sounds pitiful.

"Find some hair. There's bound to be some. It doesn't take much, not with these fancy new DNA readers. And I'll be checking for the deposit online." Silver glances at the screens. "What about the other chips I gave you? How much did they bring?"

Blake sounds almost giddy. "You won't believe it. Sixty thousand plus change. The old man had fifty thousand in his checking."

Silver whistles. "We're gonna be rich. Just keep it clean. You're wearing disguises?"

"What do you take me for?"

A meth addict. "How's your wrist?"

"The plastic insert makes it easy to slide a chip in or out without ripping skin. I put make-up in the opening, and no one even notices." Blake says.

"Find the other two boys who don't have chips. For when we're ready for them?"

Blake takes another drink. "They show up at the farmer's market every weekend toward the end."

"Where do you live?" Silver rocks back and forth in his chair."

"Kekoa didn't say. He said 'close.' Whatever that means."

Silver stands and stretches. His abs and arms are tight from weightlifting. "Okay. I'll take it from here. We can talk next when you come aboard in Honolulu and I can give you any new chips I acquire. But nose around and see if you can find out any information about the abortionist gone soft, who, and what the investigators uncover. There must be others. The more pawns to scalp, the better."

"Okay, boss. Later."

The red circle pops onto the phone, and Silver puts it down. He glances at the monitors and then calls his ex-wife. "Serenity, it's me. I'm sending you a hundred bucks to do up Melody's birthday."

"Whatever. She's four. It's not like she's going to know the difference." Serenity's voice sounds colder than an ice locker.

"Just do it. And I want pictures." Silver strokes the face on the photo of a little girl resting on the table below his giant name anchored on the back wall. It's his favorite picture of Melody. She sits on his lap at the Honolulu Honors Hotel where he took her on vacation last year.

A sigh echoes from the phone. One of a thousand different swords of guilt she loves to thrust. "Whatever."

The tramp can be so difficult. He ends the call. *Everyone has some good and some bad in them. That makes everyone equal. It's important to do something good to even the score.*

CHAPTER FOUR

Kekoa

How can I leave my family? I moan and wipe my forehead. The tropical sun leaves me dripping by the time I walk down the sidewalk on the long hill descending to Nawiliwili Bay. I pass streets lined with modest houses that cost millions. Tall, thin papaya trees line the cement brick wall next to many homes with clusters of fruit hanging from the trunk just below the spiral of leaves at the top. I can almost taste them and realize how hungry I am. Coming around a bend, I see a giant pleasure cruise ship that dwarfs the loading dock in front of it. I stop next to the sloping highway to stare at the hull and count eighteen levels. "The Golden Princess" name glows with opulence on the hull. A city on a keel. I've never been to a city—Kauai only has towns, much less see one stacked in layers. Cars rush past me, sending a breeze to remind me to get off the street.

Stepping over the guardrail, I take a shortcut through a fitness parking lot to pretend to be someone else on a ship I've never been on, to do a job I've never done. I'm the most ill-fitting person for work this ship has ever seen because this is the first job of my life. My heart races. I want to turn around and find Cliff to renege, but he'd already inserted his chip into the top of my wrist and covered the wound with a band-aid. Down the hill from the market to here, I've been preparing myself to do this, leave my family. I have to. But I can't. No. I must. For their sake. They just can't go to prison because of me. My chest aches as if the blasted ship is sitting on top of my heart.

A small stream of tourists disembarks from the ship and files out with colorful clothes, baseball caps, and wide-brimmed hats. I weave among them, and they smile at me. I appear official wearing Clint's uniform, but the pants are too short. Once I reach security, I show them Clint's badge and wave my wrist over their scanner, so they don't see the Band-Aid. My body walks onto the gangplank to the ship, but my heart stays on the dock. I plaster on a plastic grin and walk the perimeter of the boat. My smile drops away to a gape. I've only seen pictures and movies portraying cities, but this, this is a monster. Christmas tree-like lights glimmer, shouting out gold, silver, and tinsel. They almost knock me off my feet.

Curving handrails, glitz and glitter lead me to a Prada store. Women's purses, jewelry, and clothing hang like gods on pedestals. Store after store rocks my senses. I've seen a thousand sunsets in a few moments. I find the starboard side of the ship and peer out over the ocean. Tension in my shoulder relaxes a bit. *God, help me. I'm an ahi flipping around on the sand. I can't swim here.*

The usual cumulus clouds are in the sky, but I can see the sun and gauge the time. Clint said I don't have to check in until 5 p.m. It's like walking around a mall with Las Vegas in the middle. The boat doesn't even rock; it's mammoth.

I take the stairs and scope out the next level. There are oval windows. Everything is clean except for the rust in the cracks. To find my bunkroom, I take a service elevator down to the B level, into the belly of the whale.

The hallway is narrow and plain. B304, Clint said. I knock, but no one answers. I open the door. It has two bunks on each side of a small room with a desk in between up against a wall. It's about the size of our ten-foot-by-ten-foot market display. Four people have to sleep in it. Shabby curtains hang from the ceiling that pretend to cover the top bunk's length for privacy. I laugh. Privacy. I don't mind the smallness. I shared a room with my "brothers.". It's the lack of privacy and my not knowing or trusting these strangers. I feel violated already. Clothes are strewn everywhere. There are two drawers under both bottom bunks for the four tenants. I peek into the tiniest bathroom I've ever seen. The toilet is filthy, the sink has hair and brown bits in the bowl. There are four rings for bath towels, but I see the only towels hanging on ladder rungs or the floor. I pick up one off the floor. It's damp and smells like sweat. The door opens from the hallway, and a couple of men in their twenties step in.

"Who are you? What are you doing in our room with our stuff?" The short guy with an olive complexion and slanted eyes says. He presses a button on his watch, "Security one, a non-res is dressed in a ship uniform. Bring backup."

"What's his name?"

The short guy asks, "What's your name? And why are you here? Cause you're busted."

I turn to put the dirty towel anywhere except in my hand. I put it in on a bunk, but it's wet, so I try to hang it over the curtain. It falls.

"What's your name? Forget the stupid towel." He keeps talking while the taller, skinny one with black hair and light skin just stares with amusement on his face. He stands behind his friend.

"Ke," I start to say my real name and stop. My face blazes hot. It must match the color of a pig's heart before it's fried. "Clint. I work here now, and this is my room."

"That's a load of crap!" the short guy says. He puffs out his chest the way geckos blow out their throats.

His talking clock responds, "Welcome, Clint. We've been expecting you."

I stare at the watch and the guy.

The short guy moves back-and-forth sideways. One eyebrow raises above the other. He pulls his wrist closer. "Silver, this ain't anyone I've ever seen before."

Silver, the watch, or whoever is talking through it, laughs a haunting laugh, like the joke's on me.

"I know, Ferris; he's new. This is Clint. He's here to keep your toes clean. So let him."

"Alright, boss." Ferris sneers at me. He flicks his finger at my shirt. "Clint, learn to button your shirt right before you pretend to work here. All the staff can button shirts. If you're going to pretend to work here, get it right. And clean up that filthy bathroom. It's your job from now on. Every day, if it's not spotless, you're licking it clean."

I look down and flip up the bottom front of my shirt where the buttons and buttonholes overlap. Sure enough, one side is longer. Could I be any more stupid? My chest fills with indignation. I want to run to the deck and jump off, even if it's far from the water. No one in my life has made fun of me like this. At least, the water is my friend. I stop. My parents. Prison for the rest of their lives.

"So, get busy, Clintessa."

The other guy laughs.

I turn and go into the bathroom and lock the door. There isn't room to turn around without bumping into the sink. With my hand on the wall behind the toilet, I lean over and try to take deep breaths. Calm down. *God, anytime now You can tell me what to do.* How can I be Clint when I'm not?

The cabin door shuts and the sounds of men's laughter filter into the bathroom as the men stroll down the hall. I glance at the toilet, alerted by the stench. With tiny steps, I turn and open the door, rub my tummy and try not to throw up. There's a cleanser under the sink. I strip to my shorts, turn off the water in the tank, and deep dive into cleaning. Afterward, I take a shower, and someone knocks on the bathroom door.

"Hey, hurry up. I gotta pee." A deep voice sounds.

"Okay." I wipe myself with paper towels from under the sink, grab my clothes and hold them in front of me. I step out and put on my underwear, hopping on one leg. I hate being naked in front of strangers.

"Who are you?" The stocky thirty-something guy steps back.

"I'm a new staff assigned to your room to replace Clint. I'm another Clint." Pulling my pants on, I almost fall.

"The guy's real name is Blake, not Clint." He sighs as if this Blake guy is hopeless. "Where did that land mine blow off to this time?"

"Kauai, I guess." I grimace and try to get a read on whether this guy will be a friend or foe. "What's your name?"

"Peyton." He slips behind me into the bathroom. I hear, "Wow, a clean toilet," from behind the door. When he gets out, he says, "Catch you later," and flies out the door before I can ask my hundred questions.

I pop out onto the deck. By the sun, it's about two o'clock. I'm hungry, but I want to acquaint myself with the ship before I eat. I make sure my shirt is buttoned correctly. It feels weird to wear a button-down shirt. If we wore a shirt at all at home, it had to be a cotton t-shirt. Holes made it better with natural air-conditioning. Near the stairs, I find a map of the ship on an inter-actable screen and play with buttons. Thousands of people pour onto the ship, all wearing gold-hued medallions around their necks.

On deck seven, a cleaning crew with their cart loaded with towels and cleaning supplies pulls products off their cart, and I ask where to find housekeeping. A girl with an east Asian accent tells me, and I walk in to find a man sitting in a small office. A half-circle screen sits in front of him. He glances up. "You're a new face. How can I help you?"

I stand at the door. Pictures of people smiling decorate the back wall. A picture of the ocean hangs on the wall to my left; only it's a movie complete with the sounds of the ocean. The waves continue to roll onto the shore. It calms me.

"Come in. I don't have all day." His auburn hair has some white creeping around his face and beard. Some age lines show on his pale, sun-spotted face. His light blue eyes look intense, but not intimidating.

"I'm Clint. What's my cleaning schedule? And I'd like to look at my job responsibilities." Thank you, Dad, for training in careers. I hope I got the wording right.

The man's eyebrows furrow. A tray of his business cards faces me on the edge of his desk. They read "Troy MacDermott, Director of Housekeeping." He picks up what looks like a computer mouse with a read-out window and scans the back of my bandaged wrist. "Clint Ferrel." He blinks a few times and looks at me. "Blake recruited you?"

Heat creeps up my face as if I'm letting the afternoon sun bake me. "Ah, yeah, I guess."

"Well, it's odd, but as long as you get your work done, I'm okay with it." He turns and types on the center of three computer screens housed in a surrounding bronze frame. In a drawer, he pulls a watch of a drawer and hands it to me. It's similar to the one Ferris wore. I can call him using it. Two papers print off the printer on the fake wood extension of his desk to his right. "Here you go, Clint. And, this is not just a watch, it's a watchcom. An intercom, computer, and watch."

The way he said, "Clint," let me know he's figured out I am an imposter. I take the schedule and the job description. It doesn't tell me where to get my cart of supplies. "Is there someone on your staff that does a great job I could pick up ideas from? I want to do an outstanding job." Troy tilts his head and glances at me again. "Nice. You can talk to Penny. She's fast, accommodating to the tenants, and leaves nothing unturned."

"Thanks," I say and slip out the door. I've taken my turn cleaning our various rooms at home, including bathrooms, but I don't know what housekeeping does. My assigned rooms are E102-E502 port side. They are to be cleaned twice a day. I take the elevator to deck 8, Emerald. A whale of a horn blares, and I jump. The engine thrusters push the city-on-a-hull away from the dock sideways, sounding like nuts grinding, and then the engine whines and moves forward into the bay.

A holographic map of the ship by the elevator helps me find the Emerald floor. I start down the hall, and a family comes out of their room, their young children in tow. The halls are narrow. I smile. Down the hall I see a short, stocky guy staring at me, his arms crossed, a frown on his face. He waits until the family gets on the elevator and then struts toward me as if he knows me. "Clint. About time you showed up." He has baggy dark circles under his narrow eyes. He's wearing a white uniform with a name tag that says, "Silver Jacobsen, Chief of Security."

I back up a step. Something about this guy emanates evil. An evil chief of security. What an irony. He stands in front of me, smelling like cucumbers, but not real ones. Maybe it's an aftershave.

"Clint, I've been patient with you so far, but my patience has ended."

He seems anything but patient. What's this about?

"You owe me $632 from your gambling debt," Silver says. "Did you forget? If you don't get it to me by tomorrow at six, I'll have to take it out on you." He flicks my arm.

Though a head shorter than me, the man has biceps the size of my thigh. He grabs the front of my shirt and twists it, pushing me backward hard. I fall, but jump to my feet and run to the bow exit. Once on the promenade deck, I find an empty chair and sit, facing land on the port side as if I'm a passenger. What did I get myself into? I owe money to the chief of security whom I've never met, and who has to know he's never met me before. My head can't slow down long enough to make sense of it. If he knows I'm not Clint, how does he think I can get him any money? I curl up in the recliner and pull my arms over my head. I want to go home.

Clint, or Blake, tricked me into paying his gambling debts, or else Silver is making it up to scalp me. Either way, I'm screwed.

I shut my eyes and pretend I'm at home in my bed. Dinner will be ready soon, and my stomach demands food. To my brothers, aunties, uncles, and parents, I'm still somebody. They're mine. I'm theirs. My birthmother doesn't exist. Neither does Clint.

Giggles and small talk accompany the pit-pat of feet coming toward me. I look up. Some passengers stroll down the promenade dressed in suits and glittering gowns. Blast. I'd better start work. I stand and go back to the E100's hall. A cleaning cart clogs the hall at the end of the corridor while a young woman pulls supplies off it. She wears a uniform like mine. How can I get on her good side?

"Excuse me?" I call after her.

She pops into the room she's cleaning, not hearing me. Stepping in, I say, "I'm Clint, replacing another guy, Blake." Already, I feel stupid. "Can I help you while I ask you questions? I have a million questions."

"Don't want help. Stay out of my way." She keeps her gaze on the room. "Blake is a snake. Why should I trust you?"

I watch her vacuum the rectangular room. She flips the sheets up—the sheet queen at work. Next, she goes into the bathroom and throws all the towels onto the floor, and then piles them on a bath towel. Then she grabs the corners of the bottom one and stuffs them all into a big plastic bag. She tosses it outside and retrieves clean towels. Every move is quick and deliberate. The woman cranes her neck up to glare at me. "What, don't you know how to clean a room?"

I close an open suitcase next to me and brush random jewelry into a neater pile.

"What are you doing? Don't touch their things. Get out of here. Go."

"Okay, okay, I'm sorry. I'm so sorry. But where do I get a cart like this?" I back up and fall on the floor.

"The supply room. What do you think? Do you have a badge?"

I show her the white plastic picture of Clint, who must be Blake, in my pocket. He doesn't even resemble me.

"Pff," she says, glancing at the card. "Whatever. Use it to get into the door that says, 'Supply Closet.'" Sarcasm oozes from her as if I don't know how to read.

I find the supply closet and stock one of the carts in it. Dread seeps into my pores. It taunts me with my new facts. Unwanted, unworthy, unable. I push the cart to my first room and use my badge to unlock the door. A woman who is dressing screams at me, "Get out of here! Don't you even knock?"

The door slams shut in my face. I say through the door. "I'm so very sorry. It won't ever happen again. I'll clean the room later."

When I push the cart to the next room, I knock. No one answers, so I enter and clean the way the previous housekeeper modeled for me. I touch nothing that belongs to the passengers. There are cracker crumbs on the carpet. I fetch a heavy upright vacuum and make the room sparkle, which adds ten minutes to my cleaning time. The clock on the microwave before and after I clean the next room shows me it takes fifteen minutes to clean the room if I don't need to drag the clunky vacuum around. There's a small vacuum in the supply area. I switch them and finish my group of rooms. Some rooms have air conditioning blowing and some don't. I pick up a remote and push some buttons, but I can't figure it out. It blows warm. Even pushing every button doesn't make it right again. I give up and keep working another five hours. My stomach rumbles, but I'm tempted to go to bed. When I think about my roommates, I decide to figure out how to eat.

Mom and I should be cooking tonight at home. My favorite is her recipe for a pot roast cooked in the oven or crock pot all day. We doubled the recipe because my brothers and I ate two platefuls each. Tears retreat like soldiers at my will. The stock room has paper towels and trash on the floor. Instead of thinking about home, I spend a few minutes tidying. Keep positive, or I'll bury myself with sorrow, I tell myself. But missing my family oozes out of my pores and owns my soul.

I roam the restaurant area for a half-hour. The Golden Thai has gold and ivory pedestals with granite carved dragons at the entrance. Curry smells waft, inviting my mouth to water. I ask the hostess where the staff eats; she gives me a sheet of restaurants where I can eat for free. This is one. I order Peanut Pad Thai and watch couples around me. Women wear earrings, stiff hairdos, and low-cut blouses or dresses. They all wear makeup which makes their eyelashes thick and black, and their lips bright. They seem a painted version of the women who shuffled by our produce stand. My food tastes spicy, hot to my tongue, but delicious. I want to lick the plate, but no one else is.

The waitress acts like she expects a tip, but with no money on me, my smile has to make do.

I scoot out and maneuver around passengers and bump into a young woman supporting a drunk older man coming out of a bar. "I'm sorry. Please forgive me." I hold my hand up. The man smells of alcohol.

The girl, barely older than me, scowls. "Turn around," she says. The old man's forehead wrinkles in surprise, but I don't know what amuses him. She has brown hair tied back in a ponytail, and no make-up. She wears a uniform that matches mine.

I stand like an oaf for a second and stare at her, not because she's stunning, but I don't know what to do.

With her finger, she draws a circle in the air, so I turn around. She flicks down a plastic butterfly that must have been on my shoulder and steps on it. "Darn drones. Never let one ride on you again. Pornographers, thieves, and criminals use them to spy," she says.

I stare at the plastic and bend down to pick up the pieces. Its colors match my uniform. Did someone plant it on my shoulder on purpose?

Addressing me to introduce her friend, she says, "Mickey, this is—?" She puts her hand out, waiting for my answer.

"Clint," I say and shake Mickey's hand.

"Hey, man, the Mai Tais are wonderful," He slurs.

Yeah, wander full.

"Could you help me take him back to his room?" The girl says.

"Sure. What's your name?" I look at her and grab Mickey's white, leathery arm. He's a big bruiser of a guy. If he falls, she cannot help him alone.

"Lily. You new?"

"Green and looking stupid every minute I've been here," I say.

She laughs. "Thanks for helping me with Mickey. You're not looking stupid now."

I feel at home with her. "Why are you working here?"

Lily flashes up her eyebrows. "I'm saving money for college. The weather in western Washington this time of year is dreary. If I have to earn money, I might as well do it somewhere the sun shines."

I smile. "Good plan. What will you study?"

"Nursing. I like to help people." She looks at Mickey. "Are you doing okay, Mickey?"

He stumbles, but we stabilize him. Mickey says, "This is the third time I've been on a cruise. I went to Alaska, and let's see, where else did I go? Where did you say I've gone?"

Lily chuckles and shakes her head. "Mickey, I just met you. I have no idea where else you've gone."

"Oh, well. That's okay, you don't have to know. I won't tell." We get to his room, and he opens his cabin door and shuffles in, smacking his lips. When we get outside, I notice that the sky is dark, but the boat still shines like a bonfire. I'm used to being able to see the stars at night. I've joined a fake world with artificial light to replace what's real. We say goodbye and shut his door.

Lily walks with me to the elevator to go to our separate floors. "Strange things happen to drunks on the ship. I try to help them to their rooms."

I wonder what strange things she's talking about, but I'm so tired, I just say, "Anytime I can help, just ask. Goodnight."

She smiles. Gentle. Her face looks roundish with her brown hair pulled back, but she has warm, brown eyes.

I ride the elevator one level lower than hers. An invisible hammer seems to pound in my gut thinking about seeing my roommates. I knock and open the door to my room.

"Well, if it isn't Clintessa," Ferris says.

CHAPTER FIVE

Kekoa

The next morning, I awaken with my face against the ship's wall regretting getting myself into this mess. I want to wait until they're gone before I roll out of my three feet of personal space and give my life to the requirements of the ship, but I need to pee. What's the time? We don't have any portholes.

"Everyone farts." Peyton retorts.

"You don't just fart, you fumigate." Ferris has this superior voice that makes my skin crawl.

I slide out and dart to the bathroom while Ferris pulls a shirt over his head. When I come out, it stinks. "What time is it?" I ask.

Ferris sneers, "Half past puking time, time to puke again." He laughs.

Peyton says, "Five-twenty. Some restaurants open at six." He jets into the bathroom with his head hanging.

I unfold my schedule and notice that I clean at eight, but only those whose doors hold the "I'm ready to be cleaned" sign.

The guy under me is still sleeping.

When Peyton comes out, I point to the sleeping stranger and ask, "What's his name?"

"Stephen, he's a dishwasher and works late. Don't wake him up," he says. Peyton's high forehead shows more skin when his hair sticks straight up. His chunky body reminds me that eating sugar-enhanced foods the ship offers instead of the clean foods my family would serve, without enough exercise, can put on pounds. He yawns, and I almost gag from the rotten meat smell.

I pull on my old t-shirt, shorts, and slippers, and bolt out of the room before Ferris lights into me. The eighteenth floor has workout equipment and a pool. To jump on the treadmill until the sun casts its colors on the clouds sieves off some of my nervous energy, then I lean against the rail and watch. *God, I don't know who I am anymore. I'm Yours, but I don't feel like Yours. I'm nobody. Who would want to be 'Clint?'* God reminds me, "You are Mine, whatever job or chip you have." A heavy boulder I'm carrying lifts off and turns into an albatross, riding the ocean currents in my mind.

The sun throws out its color display, yellow, then orange, and finally crimson clouds feather across the sky. I'm swept in its majesty. There are no white caps on the ocean's surface, only the million little moving ripples, and there's little breeze yet. I can't see any land, only the wide expanse of seawater. A group of tourists works out on the equipment. One of them exclaims over the sunrise. I hear Spanish. Papa taught it to me as a part of my schooling, but the passengers are talking so fast, I can't understand.

My stomach churns, and I turn to go eat breakfast and change for work. My legs are longer than Clint's. People glare at my short pants. When I return, I cringe, putting on his underwear in "my" drawer, but the only clothes I brought are dirty.

I clean a couple of rooms and knock on the next. "Wait," a woman says. Then she opens the door, still buttoning up her security uniform. Her blend of shiny blond to brown hair reminds me of Canyon. Silver and gold threads blend with her hair to swirl around her face and over her shoulders. So touchable. Her face has a blank stare, but it's a perfect oval with light green eyes contrasting with her tan skin and perfect small nose. Her eyes jump out at me. Into me.

Appearing stupid is my forte. I inhale and realize my mouth is open.

"If you're here to clean—clean." She steps into the room again, grabs a bulging teal cloth bag with waves printed on it, and then walks a few feet. She turns and rubs her hand over her hips for me to see.

"Do your ovaries hurt?" I ask, not able to think why else she would stroke her hips.

She laughs so hard she bumps into the wall. I watch her long, thin legs walk down the corridor, her hips rotating. Even the security uniform can't hide her figure.

Once my heart stops pounding and my "stupid flag" comes back down again, I tear into cleaning. When I'm in the bathroom leaning over to grab the towels off the floor, I see something on my shoulder in the mirror's reflection and pull off another butterfly drone. It has a tiny camera for the eyes. I step on it and stash it in my trash bag, then put it in the trash compactor before I finish.

After my morning shift is done, I'm emptying the dirty towels for housekeeping to wash, and my badge lights up. There's a message printed on it. "Come see me ASAP. Troy Dermot, Director of Housekeeping."

I step into his office. He looks grave. "Clint, sit down. We have something to discuss." He pulls up a computer screen. "There's been three complaints of burglary in your area. This is a serious crime."

My head juts forward. I stare at Troy and stammer, "I, I didn't take anything, Sir. Please check my room, check me, whatever you need to do."

He studies me and scratches his arm.

"I found two drones, little butterflies, this big. They were on my shoulder." I stretch my fingers to show two inches.

"I know what butterfly drones are. Did you keep them?"

"No, I put them in the garbage."

"Then we have no evidence that what you're saying is true." He leans back, folds his arms across his chest, and tilts his head with his jaw moving from side to side just a bit.

His stare makes me feel naked.

"It takes a while to gather all the testimonies. I'm only in the first stage of our investigation. But I suggest you touch nothing that doesn't belong to you. We've moved the three parties out of your area to more luxurious rooms to appease them. You won't see them or know who they are, so don't try to find out." He takes a drink from his thermos. "If you find any more drones, bring them to me immediately."

"I will."

He leans forward and clicks his computer mouse. "You can leave now."

"Thanks." In my attempt to walk out the door, somehow my shoe catches on something, and I fall forward. I catch myself. Troy watches me stumble. *Lord, why do I have to be an idiot in front of everybody? Why do I have to wear shoes instead of flip-flop slippers?*

My body is heavy. One leg trudges in front of the other. I make a checklist of everything I need to do to clean a room so I don't make any mistakes. A flood of longing for home takes me like an ocean current. I fly through the rest of the rooms, ruling my mind to stay in the moment.

When my shift finishes, I eat and go to the top deck to stare over the ocean toward home. Did I leave my family in a panic over my departure? I never explained. It might be better that they don't know if I end up in jail only to be thrown into the military. Both of my aunties, uncles, and parents poured their lives into each of us boys, training us every day in their expertise. I've never been misjudged or wrongly accused before.

I shoulder my bag of dirty towels to dump into the hall when I hear a woman's voice coming from down the hall.

"Hey, towel boy. You're new. Who are you?"

I drop the towels and see the same blond I saw earlier in her security uniform coming toward me. She's about five feet seven, sort of swaying as she walks. I can't speak.

"Come on now; I know you have a name." She comes to me. Her eyes prance like Mischief's did when I'd come out of the house to throw a stick for her to catch. I'm not sure of her accent, something Scandinavian maybe, but her English is perfect.

I rub my hands up and down the outside of my thighs, thinking about what name to give. "Clint." I glance from one eye to the other.

"Clint. That's interesting. Come on; finish up. Let's go to dinner."

I stare at her and my shoulders twitch.

"Finish up. I'll wait. You're nearly done, right?"

"Yeah," I say, wondering how she knows.

I clean the last room with her looking over my shoulder. When I come out of the bathroom, I dump the towels, but forget to turn down the sheets. She waits, which makes me check my list. My face must be red, not knowing how to clean a room. I turn down the sheets and put out the mints.

"Okay, I'm done. What's your name?" I push the cart back, and she follows me.

"Ingrid. Let's go to Leonardo's for dinner. The chef is my friend."

"Okay. Staff can eat there for free?"

"No, but you can if you're with me."

I glance back at her in time to notice her smirk.

The restaurant has huge planters of shrubs out front. Inside, tan, shiny marble-looking walls reflect little stars shooting down from a giant rotating chandelier in the middle of the room with a thousand lights. Black wrought iron swirls intertwine the lights like branches. I stare.

"Come on. You look like you've never seen lights before." Her voice snaps. She sees the host seating passengers, and he nods to her. She finds a table in a corner and walks over to sit. I follow like a chick follows a hen.

She grabs the chair backing the wall. I wish I could sit facing the restaurant. Now, I'm the specimen in the middle instead of the wallflower. I rub my palms together and tap my foot.

"Calm down." She sighs. "Menu."

A holographic menu appears between us. It hangs in the air with black writing facing both directions.

"Everything is wonderful except the veal parmesan. It's tough," she says. Under the menus, a black, almost flat rectangle rests on the table. I put my hand between the menu and the box, and the menu disappears.

Ingrid shakes her head at me. I'm acting like a child in her eyes.

A server brings us water glasses. If I dare pick up a tumbler of water, I'm sure it will shake in my hand.

She laughs at me and looks at the waiter. "The usual drink. And put in an order of Lobster Linguine," she says.

He looks at me. "And you, sir?"

I clear my throat. "The same. But not the drink. I mean the same dinner."

He smiles and flashes her a knowing look.

She nods. "Menu, go." The menu disappears between us.

"Sir? What would you like to drink?"

"Just water, please."

"We have regular water, lime water, tangerine water, and Cuban Oregano water."

"Tangerine water, please."

Ingrid smiles at the waiter. "Get Clint a Mai Tai."

The waiter leaves. She twists her mouth as she looks at me. "I'm Ingrid from Las Vegas, well, originally from Sweden. Where are you from?" She unbuttons the top two buttons on her blouse. I notice a dragon tattoo imprinted on her chest.

Her smile rises more on one side of her face than on the other.

"I'm Clint, from Hawaii."

"Oh, come on now. We're both adults. No one is going to rat on you. What's your name? Where are you from?" Her voice is butter.

I adjust in my seat and notice that I'm still rubbing my hands together. "My name is Clint. I'm from Hawaii."

"Hawaii includes a lot of islands. Which did you grow up on?"

She leans forward in her chair and caresses the tabletop. Her nails remind me of pure gold, long and appearing fluid. She parts her hair on the side, and there's brown and gray at the roots and gold from an inch down, but shiny, glowing. As she tilts her head, a long spiral of gold hair falls forward into her face. "Well?"

"I grew up pig hunting in the mountains of Kauai. Most of my school years were spent in Puhi, a part of Lihue." It wasn't a lie. I studied people at the market when we sold food and flowers. "What is Sweden like?"

"Sweden has flat lands on the southeast side, where I grew up. The winters are like living in a freezer." Her voice rolls up and down as she speaks.

Our water and drinks come. She sips her pink drink with its little umbrella. My water tastes like tangerine peel, but there is something off about the flavor. It gives me a warm feeling, and I relax and let my hands rest on my lap. I sip the Mai Tai but don't trust the alcohol in it. My water glass is nearly empty now.

"So, tell me about your family."

I uncross my legs, relax, and blab everything: our private canyon, my brothers, why I ran away. My mouth yaps, almost as if I have no control. I tell her about being charged with stealing, and how I miss home. Tears run into my mouth and down my shirt. This is so unlike me.

"Give me your hand," she says and pulls something out of her purse.

My hand trembles forward, unsure where it should go.

She takes it, pokes my finger, and squeezes a big droplet of blood to the surface. With her other hand, she touches the blood to a rod that soaks it like a sponge. Then she puts a case around the rod and pushes it back into her purse.

"Why did you do that?" My voice slurs as if I'm drunk.

"Security. We have to check all our new employees to make sure they're not bringing on any diseases to the ship."

A server fills our drink glasses, and she tells him we're ready for our food now. He comes right back with it. I eat, but I'm too disoriented to notice how it tastes until I've eaten most of it. My brain seems to clear. Ingrid eats without looking at me. She checks her phone. When she's done, she takes my glass, stands, and leaves without saying goodbye.

What have I done? Why did I reveal my secrets? What will I say to my father when he gets arrested? My heart bleeds with regret.

CHAPTER SIX

Kekoa

When I return to our room, I smell the stench from the bathroom as I walk in. Someone threw up and didn't clean up the mess. Dirty underwear and dank towels lay everywhere. Dad used to make me clean up after myself. This is gross; I grit my teeth and dive in. If it stays spotless, Ferris will leave me alone. No one is in the room but me, but at least cleaning will take the edge off my failure complex. At home, I kept a diary. It helped me make sense of my thoughts and feelings, but here, I'm afraid everything I say, write, or do will be used against me.

Tucked into my cot, with my back to the riffraff of drunk roommates slurring out their rebuttals to each other, I pray silently. It's the only love I can give my family now.

And only God will love me. Roommates stagger in. The room smells of alcohol. Soon the frequent farts, belches, and snoring pollute the air. Sleep eludes me.

I sneak out into the night air in Clint's t-shirt and jean shorts and go to the bar where Lily and I met, but she's not there. The air smells like home outside. I've exchanged our private canyon for a moving Sodom—nothing is the same. Nothing except the air. The sounds of the sea slap against the ship, and the night breeze soothes me.

A middle-aged woman dressed in a white satin dress and her man in an aloha shirt pass me giggling. The ship seems to have its dimension. No one seems normal. But all I have to compare is my family. My eight pillars. My world.

The basketball court is empty. I find a ball resting in a corner and shoot some hoops in the artificial sun that never sets. To cool down, I walk the perimeter of the fifth floor. People are still up, and the bars are stuffed. It gives me time to think. I can't do anything about being accused of stealing. I didn't take anything. If I'm being framed, I'll just have to trust God to take care of me. It's not jail that worries me or getting dumped off the ship at the next port, it's ratting out my parents to Ingrid who could tell the police. That turns my stomach. Regret shreds me.

My eyelids are heavy, and I return to my room. I'm almost there when Silver walks up to me and pushes me down with his professional wrestler's beastly arms.

He says, "Where's my money? I know you've been stealing. Give it to me now." He stands over me. In the shadows, his face is difficult to make out. His cowboy boots have silver covering the pointed toes. Perfect for kicking someone's abdomen until their intestines rupture and they bleed to death internally.

I swallow. "You've got the wrong man. I didn't steal. I don't steal." By pulling my pant pockets the wrong side out, I hope to show him.

"Well, you better start." He slurs—he's been drinking. His fist rises to my face. Each of his fingers has spiked shiny rings covering the knuckles.

Passengers stroll away down the deck, oblivious. A man opens his cabin door twenty feet from us and walks our way. Silver slips off his knuckles and drops them into his pocket. He turns to the man, "Evening, Rudy. Nice night."

Rudy replies, "That you, Silver? Yeah, nice enough to go get a drink." Rudy passes and turns toward the elevators.

I step back, grab the rail, and swing over the edge. My foot finds the ledge, so I bend, grab a deck post, and hang down with my feet dangling. I'm hoping to swing to the next lower level. Silver rushes to look down at me and lifts one foot to step on my fingers. His other foot lies inches away. There's enough room between the deck floor and the base rail for just his leg to fit, so I grab his foot one hand at a time and let go of the post. The weight of my body on his foot pulls his leg out from under him. His body slams against the deck, and his leg slides out under the rail and hangs down. He tries to kick the foot I'm hanging onto. "Whoa, Baby," I say. Falling on the deck below could break some bones if I land poorly. In a flash, I see my opportunity and use it to swing. I let go of his foot as the momentum arcs me over the rail on the deck below and I roll to my feet. An elaborately dressed couple promenading toward me jumps back.

Silver screams on the deck above between growls and then swears. A wild, injured dog—with a grudge. "I'm going to kill you for this," he says. "You—Neverborn!"

I must disappear. Silver would search for me down on this floor, so I run to the bow and climb up a trellis to the level I'd just come from. In a few minutes, my watchcom begins an alarm siren. I try to silence it by pushing buttons on it but can't. I take it off. If I throw it into the sea, I can't work on the ship. But would Silver let me live after having embarrassed him? The blasted thing must receive an electronic signal. I climb up another level and look for heavy metal to hide it under. Chains or the anchor would work. I see a towel hanging over the ledge to dry, grab it, and wrap it around my watchcom. It still blares but is softer. I hear people running below me. They stop. I stand close to a cabin and press the towel and screaming device between the cabin and my body, staying still until they run again.

A Security guard says, "The fifth-floor deck is clear."

I sprint to the closed Shops of Gold. Nobody is around, so I tip back a sizeable ceramic planter enough to kick my watch under. It stops the noise. All the dirt must block the signal. Security will listen for the siren. My panting makes too much noise; I try quick shallow breaths to make less noise. While I'm trying to calm my blazing heartbeat, I realize Silver might remember me wearing a white T-shirt. I need to find another one.

There should be a security guard watching the shops at night. I don't see anyone. Maybe they've been called out to find the rogue—me.

The casino and cigar lounge is open down the hall. A few late-nighters play blackjack at a table and several people play slot machines. I slip into the smokers' area. One guy stretches out on a recliner. A gaming mask covers his face, but his head tilts to the side. He appears to be asleep, though the mask continues to play a virtual game. Finding tourist clothes and wearing a contraption like that on my face would make me invisible.

I return to the Shops of Gold and rifle through the trash bins. Sure enough, I find a dirty t-shirt wadded up and thrown away. The men's room makes a convenient place to spot wash the sweaty shirt, and change. But I'll have to have a medallion to look official. Passengers wear one, or they get kicked off the boat. Security's intercom sounds in the distance. The intercom noise stops but steps continue toward me. There's nowhere to hide except the bathroom. By squatting on a toilet seat, bent over, I wait. The guy comes in, uses the urinal, and leaves. I imagine myself kayaking and breathing in the sunrise at home to calm my trampolining heart.

When the guard heads down to the dining room, I double back to the smoking lounge, scrounging through the garbage on the way. A piece of foil from a discarded sandwich torn into strips, rolled, and braided into three strands, resembles the string part of the medallion necklace. I pull out a bottle of water from the smoker's lounge trash. By the time I finish, the sleeper on the lounge chair wakes.

"Howdy. You've been sleeping," I say.

He groans and takes off his headset. There are red marks on his forehead. "Can you tell me the time?"

"I don't know, but your medallion will probably tell you."

"Oh, yeah." He looks. "Two-thirty. Wow. I guess that game put me to sleep." He stands, stretches, and staggers toward the elevators.

I find and unfold a newspaper and lie on the recliner. The woven fabric emits cool air. With the flimsy fake medallion and cord wrapped around my neck, I cover part of my chest and neck with the newspaper and sleep with an arm over my head.

The next morning, I awaken to the sound of a whoop from the casino. It takes a bit to realize why I'm waking up in the casino's smoking lounge.

I find my watchcom under the planter. The store clerks are busy cleaning and setting up for the day, although the metal screens on the storefronts are still down. The watch isn't making noises anymore. A message flashes asking anyone who finds the watchcom to turn it into security.

Slinking back to my room, I get my uniform. Stephen snores on his back, but the rest of the guys are gone. My gut churns, and I find my way to Troy's office. I only hope Troy will believe me. Silver undoubtedly has his team looking for me. I'm trapped on a ship.

My watchcom flashes 7:30 a.m., but Troy's job as the Director of Housekeeping might start early. I knock and he mumbles, "Come in."

"Clint!" He shakes my hand when I enter, warmer than before. "Sit," he says. "I was about to message you. One of the security personnel found the items you were accused of stealing, so I'm relieved to say, you're not under investigation anymore."

My head juts forward. Mom always laughed when she surprised me, and I'd react that way. I straighten my head. "Who found it?"

Troy opens the screen and reads. "Ingrid. Well, that's it. I just thought you needed to know."

I press my hands together. "Troy, what should a person do if he thought a certain security officer was trying to pressure him into stealing?" I tap the fingertips of both hands together and sweat like a pig. My life depends on his answer and support.

"Those are serious charges. Do you have evidence?" Troy leans forward, pushing aside his breakfast sausages and eggs.

"No," I say. "No one was around when he said it. He has metal spiked finger weapons."

Troy's eyebrows raise. He strokes his chin. "Today, we're docking in Honolulu. I'll see if I can find a replacement for you. You don't have 'leave' privileges right now. If someone's setting you up, I want you out of housekeeping. Go to our restaurants and see if they need help—volunteer, or they'll just find and arrest you." He types on the keyboard, looking at the middle screen. "Okay, you're officially not working for housekeeping. Give me your badge."

I hand it over.

"I'd keep your run-in with security a secret for the time being if I were you. Rumors about bullying are circulating, but nothing has been proven. Until you have evidence, shut up, for your own safety."

The ship cruises into the harbor. I see Diamond Head's massive cliffs and towering skyscrapers as I leave. I ache for home looking at the mountain range above Honolulu. Can I jump ship and swim to shore? But Ingrid disproved my charges and saved me. She took a blood sample of me. I guess she wants to know more about me. I've never seen a woman so beautiful, so intriguing. If I can tackle a Kauai pig, I can handle a Silver pig.

CHAPTER SEVEN

Silver

S ilver watches the passengers disembark from the deck outside his office, fuming. *I'm going to kill that punk.* Nobody humiliates Silver. *Well, I assigned five security guards to find the Neverborn.* Silver smiles. *It's so easy to make use of Kekoa when the guy is a Neverborn. There's no way to trace his DNA because nobody, not even a dentist, has his records. A Neverborn can't go to a dentist or a doctor. He can be shark bait, and no one will ever know. All the crimes can point to him. What can he do?* "Jump off the boat to swim for it? He'd never make it. Or we can throw him off, and everyone is clear of any crimes. No more investigations.

Silver goes back to his monitors and watches Ingrid at the staff pool. Her body is unbelievable. He can't hear, but looking is enough, for now. Some guy is swimming in the pool. Is that Kekoa? Ingrid stalks younger men, even though she's thirty-four, Silver's age.

Silver breathes out his longing, carrying a long-winded pang and wishes she'd love him. He turns the audio to maximum on her watchcom. He watches until Ingrid's boy leaves, and she sits alone in a recliner facing the ocean, a cocktail in her hand.

"I'm going to be rich," Ingrid says and lifts her glass in the air.

Excitement buzzes through his veins. *How is she going to get rich on the ship?*

The beauty stands and walks out of the camera's range. Silver watches for where she is going. She hums, and he hears the gentle thumping of her feet on the stairs. His eyes scour the screens. His fist pounds the computer table. There. He can see her entering a coffee shop on the fifth floor. No one else shows up on the monitor next to her. She sits at a table for two and punches a number on her private phone. He can't see well because of the camera's angle and zooming doesn't help much.

"Hello." Whomever she called answers. The guy's voice sounds a lot like Kekoa's, but more mature.

"Listen. I've texted you pictures of your son, Kekoa, and of the paperwork from the blood test proving Kekoa is your son. He's seventeen now. Maili was pregnant and went for an abortion, but the doctor delivered the baby alive." Ingrid sounds thrilled and somewhat vindictive. "Your marriage to Janice won't stand up when she finds out you've had a long-standing affair with your Kauai property manager. Her father's money won't come your way anymore, either. So, if you want to keep your life from chaos, you need to send me two million dollars."

The guy doesn't say anything. He just hangs up. The click hangs in the air.

Ingrid swears in Swedish. She texts something, probably to the guy. "If his voice doesn't convince you, this should," she says to herself. She texts more and says as she types, "He likes art and swims every day. At about six feet tall, he'd be an outstanding basketball player. He doesn't have an identity chip, so he's classified as a Neverborn. The world doesn't realize he exists and doesn't need to know. He *won't* exist if you deliver your side of the bargain. Deposit two million bucks, cash, in the suitcase I send you. Lock it. Take it to the Disneyland hotel and say it belongs to room 2351. If not, KNTT news will love the story. Billionaire's son-in-law loses it all." She laughs. Then she begins a solitaire game on her phone.

Silver races down the stairs to where she's sitting. He walks up behind her. "What are you doing? That's not your cell." His hands rest on his hips. Reaching over her, he grabs it. She wrestles it back, but his arm pulls hers. He takes it and finds her last text and reads. "Ingrid, Ingrid. You've got a little high-stakes extortion going on." After a moment, he says, "Kekoa is Damian Vaskler's son? The Damian Vaskler of Excelsior Technologies. Interesting. This is the boy Blake recruited, 'Clint.' Who else knows who Kekoa is?"

"No one." Ingrid stands to face him. "I thought of it myself after I got a saliva sample and did the DNA to check his identity."

Silver whistles. "Nice detective work. You even stole someone else's phone, so you'd be untraceable?"

"I'm not stupid."

He looks into her eyes. She is about his height, but he has almost seventy-five pounds more muscle on him than she does. "I never said you were stupid. But as head of security, I'm taking this." If only he could kiss her.

She swears at him in English and calls him names he understands. Her voice becomes low and authoritative. "You have no right. The only security you're interested in is your own."

She'll pay for this. He smirks. "And what are you going to do about it?"

Taking a deep breath, her posture straightens, and she looks down her nose at him. "Wouldn't you like to know?" She gives him a stony stare.

He lets out a short puff through his nose. His lips purse. "You'd be surprised what I've figured out." Turning, he pockets her phone and walks away, hearing her swear in Swedish.

What a gold mine. He just has to persuade Damian to deposit the money into his location, not hers. He'd better call soon. Sliding back into his office chair, feels like Christmas Eve. After a glance around the monitors, he calls, giving Damian a different drop location. Kekoa turns out to be more valuable than he'd dreamed.

With gathering clouds, the night blackens apart from the moving fake star along the ocean's surface. Silver hides inside Ingrid's room. He hears her sigh from outside the door, and she brushes her wrist over the lock, opening her tiny room, her coffin. No more depression for her. No one to impress and no one to charm. That's what she gets for not loving him.

Ingrid flicks the light, but it doesn't work. "Huh," she says.

He smiles, crouching behind her bed. The door shuts behind her.

She pushes open the bathroom door and flips the switch plate. Nothing. Blackness.

His hand covers her mouth and nose with a treated washcloth until the stiffness of her body melts into his arms, and he finishes her off. If only she had loved him and included him in this extortion, she'd still be alive. It's her fault.

CHAPTER EIGHT

Kekoa

All day I look forward to seeing Ingrid again, but I can't search for her. Dishes need washing, tables bussing, and food prepped for tomorrow. My boss gives me seventy-six dollars for my share of the day's tips. The restaurant provides me with meals, but I miss Mom's cooking. We'd make More Bars for dessert so often; I can smell them cooking just thinking about them. If I go to my room, Silver's marionette-stringed pawns might turn me in, so I pile up cardboard in the stock closet for my new bedroom. Inside these four tiny walls, keeping company with boxes gets boring. After midnight, the fewest people swim and use the shower—that's over three hours from now. Taping the lock on the shower room worked, so the door never locks, but the guards come every hour.

It's like I'm the only Nene goose left in the entire world. All my species are in different dimensions. I daydream about returning home, learning logic from Dad, fencing from Uncle Tim, and mechanics from my Uncle Sam. He hauled over a Toyota Camry motor for us to take apart and put back together, and we never finished. Next year, he said we could volunteer for a mechanic friend of his on Kauai to learn how to repair cars. It's like we'll have twenty career choices if our parents have their way. It's fun. Kana and I both like putting things together and learning about cars. I'd rather drive a PlanePod though. Someday, if I ever get off this moving Reno and figure out how to get my own identity, I can.

I hunt for Lily and hawk for security as I walk up to the bar where she hangs out to help people. A tub of dirty dishes sits at a table. A busy server cleans a large table's dishes. I order a virgin margarita, and Lily prances in.

"Hey, how was your day?" I call over to her.

A smile covers her face, and she slips in beside me. "Busy." Her brown eyes tell me she missed me.

"Have you seen Ingrid? That blond from Sweden?"

Her shoulders slump a bit. "I know Ingrid. No, I haven't seen her. Why? Do you have something going on with her? She's a lot older than you."

My face feels hot. I hate the accusation in the tone of her voice. "No, but I wish I could read her. You're a girl. Is it normal for girls to be all warm and friendly one minute and distant the next?"

Lily puts her elbow on the table, and her chin rests on her hand. "Ingrid uses men to whatever advantage she can. Then she throws them away until she wants them again." Lily's eyes are sad. She glances around. "Maybe tonight isn't a good night to be here."

I want her to stay. "Why do you help people?"

She tilts her head and twists her mouth a bit in a brief smile. "I love Jesus. His love for me makes me want to help people. There are evil people on this ship. I feel it from their vibes. If I can help someone, then I'm making a difference in life. Plus, some people leaving this bar have been beaten and their chips stolen. That's why I'm here."

"I'm a Christian too. You have guts to be here. Are you ever afraid?" I glance around the room.

"Yes, but my confidence grows, even if I'm afraid." She motions to the server and orders a Pepsi.

I remember Ingrid telling me to stop helping Lily. My blond beauty must not understand how kind Lily is. The next time Ingrid comes around, I'll tell her.

Lily's hair is in a bun, but she takes it out and combs it with her fingers. It's long and silky, chestnut brown. I'm mesmerized. She notices me watching her.

"Where are you working now?" She pulls a tube of lip balm out of her pocket and puts it on. It makes her lips shiny. I never thought of her as beautiful, but tonight she is. How can I be so fickle? I'm crazy about Ingrid, but I'm still drawn to Lily.

"The Golden Crown Grill," I say. Her calm and gentle nature reminds me of Mom—so different from Ingrid and others, I see. "What do you do?"

"I take care of kids while their parents play. It's cool, but I hate when babies cry."

"I've never held a baby. I want to. They're a mystery to me."

"What?" She slaps the table. "Didn't you ever have cousins?"

"No. Just me and two brothers my age." I long to tell her everything about me, but how can I trust her?

"You poor child." She laughs. "Every child, every baby, is a miraculous adventure just beginning. I love God for making children."

"Tell me about your family." I fold my hands in front of me and lean back. She tells me about her younger brother, and how she misses him and worries about him. They'd go into the woods on Saturdays, be gone all day, and discover the world of woods together. Lily pulled him in a red wagon. They'd find dragon eggs in the creek bed and elf beards in the tree moss. By the time she tells me about the story she made up to explain the frog's croak, I know I want to learn everything about her.

"What makes you tick?" She says and leans forward. Her hand rests on the table, showing her long fingers with rounded medium-length nails—soft, unpainted, clean, gentle, and real. I want to touch them.

"I love sports of every kind, especially basketball. Pig hunting jazzes me, swimming in the ocean, and surfing. Some job where I can help people: be a doctor, a firefighter, or a counselor like my mom someday."

The pupils in her eyes are big, making her eyes so warm and beautiful. Neither of us says anything. We just stare at each other, basking in the treasure we've just found. A warmth flows through me, like drinking a mug full of Mama's orange-spiced tea.

An old guy at the bar with an aloha shirt on starts slurring the words to the song playing in the background. I look at Lily and her whole face smiles. We rise together and approach him. I say, "Hey, friend, can we walk you to your cabin? The bar will close soon."

He giggles, "You children shouldn't be in a bar." He can't pronounce "children." It comes out like "ch-chillin."

"Well, Grandpa, we are, so we can help you back, then we'll go to our rooms like obedient children," Lily says. She sits next to him.

"What if I don't want to walk to my room?" he says, facing me.

I look at Lily, not sure what to say.

She smiles at me as if to say, "I've got this one."

Lily faces the man. "What's your name? My name is Lily, and this is Clint," she says and puts a hand on his arm.

"How, how do you do?" He drinks from his glass. "I'm Leroy, Leroy from Kansas City."

She taps his arm. "Leroy, are you a Chief's fan? Do you watch football?"

"Yes, siree. I do." He takes another drink and empties his glass.

Lily pats his arm again. "Leroy, the game's over. It's time to go home. We won."

"Oh my, we did?" he asks.

I laugh.

"Yes, and you won a free trip to your cabin accompanied by us. We're here to make sure you get to your room safely."

The inset lighting above the bar highlights Lily's hair fluttering over her shoulders as the trade winds blow into the open bar. She has a perfect profile, like Aunt Cindy. Perhaps Auntie looked like this when Uncle Tim married her—cute.

"Okay," he says.

Lily turns to the bartender. "Can you close out his bill?"

He lifts the drink he's made. "Sure enough."

Lily asks Leroy, "Where's your wife? Are you married?"

Leroy wobbles off the bar stool, takes Lily's arm, and says, "She went to the art gallery with her friend. P-p-probably in the room by now."

I see security looking around, so I duck down behind Leroy and Lily.

Lily says, "Clint, what are you doing?"

"Go," I say, and crawl to the bathroom door five feet away to duck in. There's no one there, so I enter the only stall with a door and crouch on the toilet with my feet on the seat. I didn't shut the bathroom door, so I can hear.

Glasses clank, and a male guard ask Lily, "Have you seen Clint?"

She says as smooth as ice cream, "Hey, he likes to play basketball at this time of evening. You might try the court."

I sigh and sneak a peek out of the door. The guards, Lily, and Leroy, scurry away.

The bartender could push the security button on his watchcom and notify them I'm there if he sees me. If I had clothes to disguise myself, I might be able to sneak away, but all I have is one t-shirt and black pants.

A man comes in to use the urinal. I stay hidden, crouching on the toilet seat. My knees hurt from the deep knee-bend position. He leaves and someone else comes in. I hear him just outside the stall door I'm in. He knocks and says, "Hey, you comin' out any time soon? The girls might not like me going into their bathroom."

I flush and open the door. "Sure." When he comes out, I say, "Hey, could you check lost and found and see if there are any pants or shirts I could wear? I hate walking in public with a hole in my britches."

He looks at me and nods, "Whatever, dude."

A few minutes after he left the bathroom, he opens the door and throws a pile of clothes on the floor. "There you go." The door closes.

I grab the clothes, an overcoat too heavy for the tropics, a shirt someone threw up on, long pants, and an empty wallet—that all stink. The wastebasket has an extra bag under the open one at the bottom for me to put my clothes in, a trick I know from housekeeping. I put on the shirt, pants, and overcoat. The pants are too big, so I stuff wadded paper towels in the front. I look fat.

The bartender goes in the back to get something, so I stroll out of the room as if I'm legit.

Once I'm at my restaurant, the night manager is about to lock up for the night. He wrinkles his nose as I walk by but only says, "About time. I was just locking up. If you're going to sleep here, get here before I leave."

"Thanks," I mumble.

"What's with the Sherlock Holmes outfit?"

"Lost and found had it. I'll wash everything and have an extra set of clothes for when mine needs washing."

He nods his head and sniffs. "Oh, yeah. Well, see you tomorrow." He pulls down the metal grate and locks it.

CHAPTER NINE

Silver

Silver paces his office. He thinks better on his feet. His lower back hurts from his professional wrestling days. He could retire and never need to go back to work again if this gig works out. The air conditioning can't keep up with the heat, so he turns it up by speaking to the echo device. "Siri, turn up the air conditioner."

Colder air whirrs from the vents around the floor.

He has to admit to himself that Ingrid surprised him, investigating the new Clint all on her own, keeping it a secret from him. Her loss. Losing her life. But he gave her kudos for figuring it all out. Now, he has to get Damian on board to pay the two million dollars to his offshore account in the Bahamas. He got up at five to come in and make the call at 8 a.m. west coast time.

"Good morning, Damian speaking."

Silver wiggles his fingers. "Damian, we're holding your son, Kekoa. Did you get the previous message and pictures of him?"

Irritation shows in his voice, "There is no alias 'son.' I have three kids by Janice. I'm happily married. Never call me again."

"Janice doesn't know about Maili. She's going to get a package, as is your father-in-law, if you don't cooperate. Did you listen to your son in the message? He sounds just like you. Your son has AB-negative blood. That wouldn't be yours, would it?"

A heavy sigh filters through the phone. "She had an abortion. This isn't possible."

"Well, that could be what she thought. Google 'Kauai Abortionist Turns on Patients.' You'll be surprised."

Silver hears a door shut. "Damian, I'm going out for coffee. Want your usual?" A woman's sexy voice comes through the phone.

"No." Damian pauses. "Yes, the usual. Cancel my appointments for the day before you go."

She sounds shocked. "Okay. Can I help in any way?"

"No," he says to her. Damian waits a bit before speaking again. Maybe he is looking up the news article about the abortionist on his computer. "Whoever you are. What if this fetus did live? If I get you your two mil, who's saying this kid doesn't pop up next year and the next?"

Silver sinks into his air-conditioned chair. "I will guarantee that no one will ever see him again. I'll send you pictures of his corpse."

Damian swears. "Murder. Must it come down to murder?" He pauses. "Yes, I guess it does. I've answered my own question. This baby should have never been born."

"Exactly." Silver says. "I want you to wire the money to a different place."

"Wait. I don't have two million sitting around. I'll need at least a week to gather it."

Silver flares his nostrils and blinks. "One week. That's it. If the money isn't in the account, everyone gets a certified package, and then social media videos, and other secret ways I have invented to get the word out."

"Okay. But I need proof of the death before I pay," Damian yells.

Silver smiles. "You will."

Silver stands and walks out onto the deck to stare at the ocean. He has a new life to plan. Nothing on the ship matters anymore, only Kekoa's death.

CHAPTER TEN

Kekoa

The ship pulls into Maui's Kahului Harbor with riveting mountains that divide to make a "v" between the two ranges against the blue sky. I lean over the deck rail and wish I could disembark and explore the island. Security would arrest me on sight. I notice police officers boarding before any passengers are allowed off. Everyone seems impatient to disembark, but security won't let them. Then two security guards carry down someone covered on a stretcher. The masses pour out once the corpse is in a black van and drives away.

The city doesn't appeal to me, not one as massive as Honolulu. It's a concrete monument to commercialism. A wave of homesickness guts me. The Maui mountains look the same as on our island. Puffy clouds chug across the sky. I turn and go back to the restaurant.

My manager bends over inventorying the bottles behind the bar.

"Hey, need some extra cleaning done?" I offer. Staying busy might keep me sane.

"Yes, matter-of-fact. You can start by wiping down all the chairs and tables. I'll fix you lobster and steak for lunch."

"Yum. Can I watch?"

"Sure. You like to cook?"

"I do. Mama and I would cook dinner every third day. We always had pork or chicken, though. It was free."

"Oh, so that's why you love beef."

I laugh. "Well, I'm almost ready for pork again, but just for a meal or two. Hey, I just saw a dead body being carried off. Do you know anything about it?"

He stands. "No, but I'll keep my ear to the ground."

"To the sea, you mean."

Stayton chuckles. "You're seventeen, but honestly, you're the best worker I've had in years. Don't tell anyone I said that. And I won't be able to even pay you a salary until you get a chip. I can't believe after knowing you a bit that you've done the crimes you're accused of."

A pit in my gut forms like a punch. "I can't believe there are people who commit crimes and then find people to take the blame."

Stayton put down the phone he uses to track his inventory. "Welcome to the real world."

A stir from the hallway brings our eyes up from our work. A police officer pops into a restaurant across the way. I crawl to the bar and worm my way behind it to the other side.

Stayton whispers to me, "He's coming this way. There's a laundry basket to your left. Crawl in it."

I look to see the tall plastic laundry basket with a cloth bag wrapped inside it and folded neatly over the top. How do I crawl into it without standing or making noise?

"What can I do for you?" Stayton asks.

An unfamiliar voice says, "We have to search the floor for an unauthorized young man, six feet tall, has some Hawaiian blood by his appearance, goes by, 'Clint.' Have you seen anyone answering that description?"

Stayton's voice is expressive, too expressive. "What? No, really? What did he do?"

Another voice sounds deeper. "Possibly murder. We're required to search your area."

"Sure, go right ahead." Stayton's voice seems to trail off.

I turn the basket sideways and crawl in feet first, but have to make it tip upright, which will make a noise. I tell myself to breathe. My chest doesn't seem to know what to do, breathing with shallow, quick breaths. The hair on my neck feels like it's sticking straight up.

"Gentlemen, can I make you my special drink?" He sounds a little off. "Murder. Wow. We need you to catch this guy before he kills anyone else. It's on the house. Mocha, Frappuccino, or something stronger?" He comes next to me and lifts my basket upright, fluffing a few bar towels over my head.

"Nah, I have acid reflux. I have to lay off coffee." The man's deep voice grows fainter. He must be going into the storage room.

"Yeah, sure, I'll have a mocha," the other one says, his voice coming from the other direction, toward the kitchen.

The man returns from the storage room. He says, "You been sleeping in your storage room?"

Stayton clanks a coffee pot. "I work till two in the morning. It's so much easier to lie down, catch a few hours, and start the donut dough at four. You ever work in the restaurant industry?"

"Sure did." He grumbles. "I hated it. Grease in my hair, my clothes smell like food from yesterday's trash can."

Stayton fakes a laugh. "You nailed it." He calls out, "Here's your mocha."

The other officer's voice became louder. "Um, smells ono." He slurps. "Nice and creamy."

"Where are you guys from?" Stayton asks.

"Hilo on the Big Island," the deep-voiced man says.

The perfume from the dryer sheets used to dry the towels makes me want to sneeze. I pinch my nose to stifle it, but my head explodes anyway. "Cachoooo." My heart drops to the floor.

"Well, well," the guard says, pulling off towels and clanking what I think are handcuffs sounds.

I try to jump out of the basket, but it falls over. An arm holds me like a granite slab—I'm done.

They put handcuffs on my wrists behind my back and shove me forward. "Boy, after what you have done, prison is too good for you. We all liked Ingrid."

I stumble, and the corner of a table jabs into my gut. I'd like to defend myself, but my accusers seem to have made up their minds already. Stayton doesn't look at me. His eyes are on the bar he's wiping down.

"Silver said to keep him out of public view."

The guard's name tag says, "Kai." He grabs a tablecloth from the bottom of the hamper, drapes it over my shoulders, and ties it in the front, concealing my handcuffs. He holds my arm and guides me through the eating area and down the service elevator. The other man follows a step behind us. We walk single file down the narrow hall on the second floor and stop at 218. Kai opens the door and pushes me to the floor. My hands scream to pull loose and protect me, but the cuffs hold them captive. Something on the way down hits my shoulder, and my face plants into the dirty carpet. The door slams shut, and the lock clicks.

It's dark. The rough carpet wreaks of dust, vomit, and mildew. This must be the brig where they hold passengers too drunk to function. I stand to my feet and creep along the walls to determine the contents of the room. After two steps, I almost trip over a toilet. As I slide my arms against the wall, I search for the light switch, but can't find one. The slabs of a bedframe are there, but no padding or sheets. A tiny sink sits next to the toilet. I try using my mouth to turn it on and then spit and rinse my mouth with water for a minute. If this is the only way I can get a drink of water, someone else has had to do it too. The stench from the toilet tells me nothing in the room had been cleaned in a very long time.

Once I have a layout of the room, I sit on the bed. Anyone else in my family would be praying now. A cloud of questions buzz around me like stinging bees. Is Silver framing me for murder? Why did the security guard say, "We all liked Ingrid?" Did something happen to her? I remember the playfulness in her eyes when she drew me in, and then the indifference when she wanted to leave.

If girls at the farmer's market smiled at me, my insides somersaulted with joy. How I longed to spend hours, days, and weeks listening to these beautiful creatures called "women." Now, I'm on a ship full of them, and I long to go home and never leave. I want a hug from my mom the most. Her reassuring words and gentle strokes of my hair soothed me, even when I ripped my skin on the rocks surfing or got food poisoning from a vendor at the market. But I have no home anymore. I was never born. Living with my family only endangers them.

I lie down and curl on my side. My wrists hurt from jerking against them so hard, and my back and shoulders ache from having my hands held behind my back. With my eyes closed, I listen to the sounds of the ship. As a backdrop, the hum drones from the massive engines and airflow from what must be a vent. Two women talk in Filipino as they walk by. I lean against each wall in the cell and listen. My stomach churns and rumbles. How long before I can eat? What will happen if they take a blood sample and find out I'm nobody? But what happens if I'm a stooge for whatever Clint does? *God, I remember King David holed up in a cave. King Saul wanted his life. Maybe he felt like this. Or Jesus, beaten and mocked, knowing He would have to die to save His family—including me.*

I don't know how to die for my family. They seem an ocean away. In my mind, I can see sharks swimming toward me, ready to tear me to bits and fill the seawater with my blood. My hope sinks to the bottom, and I sway with the seaweed in silence.

After a while, there are thumping sounds from someone walking down the hall. Sidestepping around the room, I press my ears to the wall. Behind the toilet, there's a flush, some whistling, and then a door shuts.

On the opposite side, two women talk on the other side of the wall. "Where should we go to dinner?" one says.

"The usual. I'll go for the teriyaki chicken. Hey, did you hear about the dead body?"

"Yeah. That blond bombshell who works in security. Well, who *worked* in security," the other says.

If I yell for help, what will they do? Call Security, who will come and punch me? The women must be talking about Ingrid.

One of them says, "You never know about these security twits. They're the weirdest security I've ever seen. We've had more passengers complain about thefts than on my other gigs. And the woman who died, she was the most 'unsecurity' woman you could imagine, dressing in a uniform too small for her, flirting with all the good-looking men half her age."

"Yeah, who would trust her?"

"Blimey, the bigger question—who killed her?" Says the other as the sound of a door shutting ends my eavesdropping.

Ingrid. Killed. I lie down again to fathom the implications. Murder. And I'm the one being framed for it.

CHAPTER ELEVEN

Kekoa

Time torments when you're sitting in the dark. As if I'm invisible in a dark room and the demons pinch my heart, saying, "Forgotten. Unloved. Unwanted." I think of all the things I wish I'd said to my family, the stupid things I regret doing and saying.

The ship should head toward Nawilliwilli Boat Harbor soon. My chest shrinks, almost squeezing tears out of my eyes. Home. If only I could get out of this jail and jump ship. I could live in the jungle or work as a dishwasher in the sunny southern town of Poipu and just get tips. Anything but being a pawn for someone else's crimes. *God, help me.* A tiny vapor of hope drifts into me, but a review of the facts dispels all hope. My aching wrists and stabbing shoulder blades bring reality.

In the night, a faint knocking sound at the door wakes me. In the blackness, I jump to my feet, which jerks my bloody wrists against the sharp edges of the cuffs. I sit on the bedframe, out of balance. Someone expects me to open it. A click sounds and a whoosh of ocean air rushes in. Dread fills my carcass, creeping through the dark like a centipede.

"Dang, it's dark in here. Kekoa, come on. Sh. Quiet." It's Lily's voice.

I stammer, "How—"

"Sh, come on." She grabs my arm.

The dim light from the hall blinds me as if I'm staring at the sun. Leaning against the door frame helps steady me.

"You okay?" Her hand squeezes my arm.

"I can't see. Too bright." My eyes can open a bit now.

"You'll be okay." She closes the door and half drags me down the hall toward the elevator, the only way off the floor since we're in the ship's belly.

I stumble, and she steadies me. But by the time we arrive at the empty elevator, I'm able to open my eyes.

"Wait," she says. "What floor is the supply closet on? Maybe there will be something there to at least hide your cuffs."

We scurry off floor five. A couple passes us going in the other direction, but they've had too much to drink to notice my hands are bound behind me. Once we're at the supply room, Lily swipes Ingrid's badge over the lock and opens the door.

"Where did you find that?"

She smiles, "Necessity. I popped down to security to see whose dead body everyone was talking about and saw it on Silver's table. Well, truth be told, I paid for a couple of drinks to be delivered to his office an hour before I went. He was in the bathroom as I'd hoped and prayed, so I took the badge."

The door pushes in, and we turn on the light and ease the door shut. We both wander around the room but find nothing amid the cleaning solutions, towels, and sheets to either hide my hands or break open my shackles. An enormous container of trash that someone didn't bother to take to the compactor sits in a corner.

Lily sees where I'm looking. "Trash. I hope there's something in it." She has faith enough for both of us. She opens it, and I watch while she digs. The serious expression she wears turns to a smile. Out of the bag comes an ugly, large, women's black sweater. She puts it around my shoulders and buttons one hole in the front.

I'm not sure if she's mocking me or not.

Standing on her tiptoes, she ruffles the loose curls in my hair. "Wait, I saw …" She digs in a box behind some towels and brings out lipstick and mascara and paints my lips. Some pink powder she finds makes my cheeks rosy.

"Hold still." She brushes my eyelashes with a black goop.

I shake my head.

"Hold still."

I'm a doll being dressed, not even a man anymore. I say, "Are you making fun of me?" My heart is ready to be fried.

"No." She steps back. "You are now a cross-dresser. No one will recognize you." She smiles. "Great. Just bend your arms so they don't hang down lower than the sweater."

I hope she's not embarrassing me on purpose.

"Okay, let's go." She opens the door.

It's dark outside, almost dawn by the peak of light on the horizon when we step out onto the deck, except the ship has enough lights for a city. We sit in a couple of chairs overlooking the ocean impersonating tourists. At some point, security will come for me in the brig and realize I'm gone. Then another search will ensue.

"Where can we hide?" Fear eats at the edges of Lily's voice.

"In the lifeboats," I say without thinking about it first.

"We have to break off your handcuffs. Any ideas?"

I moan. The cuffs cripple me. Am I setting up Lily to be a criminal now by helping me? "It's no good. I'm just going to get you into trouble."

Her hand rests on my arm. "We both love God. If you don't believe in yourself with God *in* you, then trust in Him."

"I'm nobody. Nobody wants me."

"But you've talked about your dad and mom. I'm confused."

"Yeah, but I found out they're not related to me at all. My real mom didn't want me." This isn't the time to get into all of this, and I've already betrayed my family enough by talking about them.

Lily puts her hand on my arm. "There's God, who laid down His life for you. And me. I'm risking my future on this ship because I want to be your friend."

I stare at her. Her gentle brown eyes encompass me, and warmth fills me. "Thank you," I say, but can I trust her? Did Silver give her Ingrid's badge to further implicate me?

After a few moments, she says, "Right now, we've got to figure out what to do. God, tell us what to do." She says, "Can we crawl into a lifeboat?"

I look around the area. If they had not shackled me, I could shinny down the launch bar and pull myself under the cover, but I can't even walk naturally now. *Okay, God, please help us.* "I don't know. Right now, we need to stay out of sight."

Lily presses her lips together, staring out at the sea.

The long silence drags out my despair.

"I know," she says. "Rupert."

"Rupert?" Is it a dog, a person, somebody's pet chicken?

"He's one of the regulars at the bar. Has dementia, I think. I help him return to his room all the time. Let's visit him." She takes my arm as if we're in love, puts on her happy face, and we walk the deck. To my surprise, no one even stares at me. I want to look in the mirror, but then I don't want to. We jump on the elevator and go up to the eleventh floor. She knocks on his door, but no one answers.

"Dang. He's probably gone to breakfast," she says. After looking in both directions, she pulls out Ingrid's badge and passes it over the door lock. It clicks, and she pushes it open and turns on the light. "Stay here until I come for you." The door closes.

CHAPTER TWELVE

Kekoa

In Rupert's room, clothes cover the floor and stick out from under the bed, maybe by accident if he comes in drunk. A lamp is on the floor like someone has knocked it off. On the table, a drawing pad with pictures of birds lies open with a pencil and colored pencils resting next to it. He's drawn an egret that looks decent. On my left, a small bathroom door is ajar. I turn my back to the light switch and struggle to turn on the light with my hands behind my back. It hurts to bend my cut and bruised wrists. I give up. On the table, I remember seeing the pencil. Biting it, after many tries, I turn on the light with it.

My face looks like a girl's. The mascara makes my eyes huge. If it weren't for my thick neck and muscled shoulders and beard stubble, someone might think me female.

A fascination equals my disgust. I don't want to be pretty. My mind plays out how Canyon and Kana would taunt me if they saw it, and I want to wipe it off using the only hanging towel. But another part of me thinks it's brilliant, and Lily would be disgusted if I wipe away my cover. My full lips shine, so kissable if they were on a girl. My five o'clock shadow reminds me of Mom. I'd tease her by rubbing my cheek against hers, and she would push me away and snap her cotton kitchen towel at me until I left to shave.

I sit on the bathtub's edge, immersed in the memory of Mom's love.

A knock on the door sends me to my feet. I don't know what to do. "Housekeeping," a woman's voice says. The door opens and someone shuffles around in the room.

After glancing at the mirror, knowing the housekeeper will realize I don't belong, I say, "Just straighten and leave the towels on the bed. I'm in the bathroom."

A woman's voice says, "How aw you today, Wupert?" She sounds Asian.

She knows who he is? Some older folks, I'd heard, live on cruise boats. It's cheaper than rest homes. I struggle to guess specific details about Rupert—what phrases an old man might like to use, and how he would sound. "Fine, mighty fine," I say in my old-man voice.

"Can you hand out the used towels for me?"

No, my hands are tied at the moment. Literally. I stare at the distorted version of myself in the mirror. Who am I?

She persists. "Throw the towels on the floor outside the bafwoom."

"Okay," I say and push the flush handle with my foot.

Kicking the towels together on the floor makes me lose my balance. I can't pull my hand out to catch myself, and the impulse tears at my wrist. My head hits the shower wall and I fall, pulling the shower curtain down with me.

"Are you alwight?" she says. Concern seeps from her voice. "Shall I come and help you?"

"No," I remember. I need to sound old. "No, dear. I'm not dressed. Turn around, and I'll kick the towels out." You idiot, why did you say, "kick?"

"Awight. I turn awound." She sounds fainter as if she has turned.

I roll over, get to my feet, and slide the stupid towels sideways toward the door. To open the door, my hands must be at level with the doorknob. I face the toilet and bend over so my hands can twist the knob. Then I can kick the linens out, balancing on one leg. The girl with a black bun on the back of her head says, "Sank you." I bang the door shut with my head. Functioning without hands exhausts me. Did she see my handcuffs?

In a minute, her cart rumbles down the corridor away from me.

Putting up a shower curtain with no hands is impossible. I hope Lily can.

I have to pee. It's so hard to work your pants against the wall until they've slid down enough, and it takes more effort to pull them back up again—without hands.

When Lily and Rupert come back, I've gotten my pants up, covering my privates at least.

"Kekoa?" Lily calls.

"I'm in the bathroom. Don't come in." I glance in the mirror and view my watermelon-red face. "Send Rupert in."

Rupert pokes his head into the bathroom. "What the hallelujah happened here?" He looks around, but his cane doesn't work well in the cramped space. Rupert's hand grabs the sink cabinet to steady himself. Bent over, I see the top of his busy white hair and the shiny bald center reflecting the light on the ceiling. Hair comes out of his nose and ears like his head is full of it when he looks up at me.

His eyes seem to crawl over my ruby lips, curls, and pants half down. With disgust, he says, "What kind of man are you? And why are you in my room? Get out."

Lily comes in, sees me, and says, "Oops. I didn't see anything."

"Go!" I yell at her.

"You go." Rupert snarls at me, thinking I'm yelling at him.

Lily laughs. She sits on the bed, leaning forward, roaring, and then slides to the floor, unable to stop. Rupert sees her and starts laughing too. I can't help myself. I peer in the mirror and laugh until I cry. It takes a minute for us all to stop. Once someone stops, someone else starts again, and we all catch the hysteria once more. It feels good to laugh as if heaven has reached down and taken my load for a few minutes. When we all control ourselves, I say, "Lily, if I stay turned around, please come in and pull my pants up with your eyes closed. I can't without hands."

Rupert looks at my disappearing arms. "You don't have any hands?"

Lily can't get in. One person fills the bathroom. Three won't work.

"Rupert, can you step out for a second? Kekoa needs some help. His hands don't work," Lily says.

He steps out. I turn around, and her warm hands touch my arm. Then where my hips are and follows to pull up my shorts. I turn around.

"You can open your eyes now," I say. I watch her beautiful eyes open inches from my face. My embarrassment is gone, replaced by a driving thirst to be close to her forever. Her eyes find mine. Those soft fingertips glide up my arms to my shoulders. I want to kiss her and pull her into my arms, but my hands are bound. She smiles, turns, and fixes the shower curtain.

I want to kiss her.

"Okay," she says, and I follow her out. "Rupert, this is Kekoa. He's a man, but I put make-up on him to disguise him."

The old man's wrinkled brows seem to meet in the middle, with white whiskers poking out like the top of a cactus.

"Is there a costume party on the ship?" he asks.

Lily's eyes twinkle. "There is." She whispers to me, "somewhere."

Housekeeping made up Rupert's bed and folded the clothes that fell on the floor. A mint lies on his pillow, and the bed is made perfectly. The lamp stands in its rightful place, no longer on the floor.

"Well, what time is it?" Lily looks at her watchcom.

I stare at it on her wrist. "Don't you want to get rid of it? They can track you with it."

Lily stares at it. "Oh, yeah. I guess they haven't put two and two together yet."

We both stare at Rupert, who is sitting on his bed looking exhausted.

Lily puts her hand on his arm. "Do you need a nap, Rupert? Do you want us to go?"

He yawns, smacks his lips, and curls his knees up. "You can go if you're hungry, but I like the company. You can color if you want to. Don't get old. Do what you want. Just don't get old." His eyes close.

Lily takes my hand. "What's the plan? Please tell me you have a plan."

"Did Rupert pack any metal cutters?" I ask.

"Don't I wish?" She sits on the floor, tapping her fingers against her crisscrossed legs.

The silence hangs in the room like a London fog on a fall night. Rupert snores, which might have been funny, but the wave of lightheartedness has passed. Our lives hang in Silver's spider web. I lean against the door because there is no place to sit. My wrists are bleeding again, but I don't want Lily to see.

"What time is it?" I ask. We're heading to Kauai. If we jump ship, at least we'll be away from Silver.

Lily taps the watch. "Oh, yeah. I'd better get rid of it. It's a few minutes before seven o'clock." She takes it off and swings it around.

I kneel next to her and lean over to whisper in her ear, "Yeah, in case it can hear. They may have seen you in a video taking Ingrid's badge or helping me down the corridor. Please get rid of it."

She looks at me. Her face is only inches away.

My breathing eases, and warmth seeps into my body like when I slip into our hot tub after a winter dip in the stream. I stand.

A smile ghosts on Lily's face. She gets up and walks out the door.

She returns. "I threw it in the ocean."

"Could you see the lights of Lihue?"

"It's raining. All is gray." Her face is crestfallen.

I long to put my arm out and pull her into a hug and imagine her melting into me. "Hey, you." My feet move close to her. She looks up at my face. I bend down and kiss her forehead. Her arms wrap around me. I've never felt so protective of anyone in my life. She must feel my heart pounding, but her fingers stroking my back are more soothing than hugging Mischief. I don't want to pull away.

"What do we do?" she asks. The desperation in her voice pulls my heart back to make my head think.

"I can swim for it. Are you a swimmer?" I lay my head against the top of hers.

She pulls away a bit and looks up. "You can't swim with your arms bound."

"Maybe I can." I smile and realize—my mouth spread lipstick all over her hair. I can't even hug right.

"When Ingrid took me swimming in the staff pool, there were float devices. In the lost and found, I vaguely remember some fins and mouthpieces. Have you gone?"

She pulls away when I say, "Ingrid." You idiot. Don't talk about Ingrid. "I . . . please don't think. . . I've never dated or kissed *anyone*." My face folds into a frown. "I'm a three-year-old with girls. I grew up with three brothers and no sisters. We home-schooled. Our church consisted of our families."

"Did you ever kiss Ingrid?" Her eyes reach into me, waiting for an answer.

"No," I say. "She seemed so friendly. I needed a friend."

"I remember. You wanted me to help you get her to like you. You don't get it. She was a tease—an animal, seeking to devour."

"You're probably right. But I didn't want her to die," I say.

Lily nods and looks down. "Yeah, I've been there. I'll investigate." She ruffles my hair and leaves. Rupert rolls over. A couple walks down the hallway outside the cabin door and chats about a show they'd been to. Heaviness fills me. What will happen if they catch Lily?

CHAPTER THIRTEEN

Lily

I swing my arms and give a leery smile, walking past a couple of young women down the narrow corridor, pretending my life hasn't gone haywire. My feet slap as I walk. Light shines up through the flooring, giving a soft glow to the peach hall without being bright. Everything about the cruise ship is commercial—twenty-four-hour slot machines, shops open at night. The expectations of passengers thinking they can buy happiness or love by coming on a cruise bothers me. Worst of all, the crime that oozes all around, hardly seen, swept away. People wake up and find their chips missing. A crook scans the chips of people too drunk to notice while it's still in their wrists and empties their bank accounts. When they try to make a purchase, the merchandiser declines them.

I'm afraid of Silver. His ego goes before him like the way an invisible demon intimidates and defuses all goodness.

The elevator is full. I sense the Lord telling me to take the stairs, anyway. The rain falls in light, lukewarm drops. I don't have dry clothes to change into, but what will it matter if we're going to swim to Kauai, anyway? I need to find a swimsuit while I'm at lost and found and not take the risk of going to my room. Fat chance of finding one that fits.

It takes a while to go up level after level. I stop and rest. Has my childcare team missed me yet? This is the first shift working as a babysitter I've missed since I started six months ago. Without a job reference, it will be harder to get a position wherever I land after this.

A security guard comes toward me. His eyes stare at me. Pounding my feet, I run up to the next level and pop in. It's all cabins. Where can I hide? I've thrown my watchcom into the ocean. What else could they be tracking? Of course, Ingrid's badge. I stew for a few minutes and run down the corridor. A family comes toward me, pushing a baby stroller. Perfect. I slide it out of my pocket. "Oh, isn't she a darling?" I bend over the air-conditioned satin-lined stroller. The sweet infant is a few months old kicking in her pink onesie.

The dad stops to show off his darling. He must have caught my huge grin.

"She looks like a cherub now. But she's been wailing for hours. What were we thinking? My mom was going to watch her, but she got sick," he says.

"Well, there's 'Babysitter Cruise,' a babysitting service on the fifth floor." The darling baby has big blue eyes and sweetheart lips. Little wispy white-blond curls frame her face. I wish I could take her home. The parents may have selected these traits with a gene selection program.

The brown-eyed dad brightens. "Really?"

I slip the badge into the stroller and stroke the baby's face and say, "Yeah. Hey, gotta go, I'm late." Sprinting to the other side, I go in the opposite direction as the stroller. The hallway is straight. Security can see me. *Lord, what do I do now?* My brain thinks of the restaurant Kekoa works in. He trusts the manager.

It's mid-morning now. I make my way to the restaurant, not seeing any security. Stayton is cleaning. A few customers are eating breakfast, some are eating lunch around the room.

"Stayton, can I talk to you?" Then I whisper, "I'm with Kekoa."

"Sure." He pours water and ice into a glass and sets it on the bar. His eyes flit about as if he's being watched.

"What can I get you?" He writes something behind the bar and lays a napkin out next to my drink. It says, "I'm sure

Silver is recording us. How is Kekoa? Just give me a star or frown."

"I'll have a virgin margarita. A five-star margarita."

He makes it for me and pretends to scan my wrist for payment. He charges me five cents. I laugh.

Stayton's eyes study me, so I press my wrists together and tuck my hands under my chin, my elbows on the table, and say, "Any ideas?"

"I caught that gleam in your eye. The only way to set you free is to know the passcode."

Passcode. What is he talking about? I realize he's talking about the handcuffs after all. It takes a code, not a key to open Kekoa's handcuffs. "Do you have any ideas for our trip—equipment, advice?" I keep my voice low.

He wipes the already clean counter in front of me. "Kauai. We should arrive in a few hours. Beautiful island." He makes the rounds with his water pitcher filling passengers' glasses. I take my drink and leave.

When I get back to the room, my knocking wakes up Rupert taking his after-breakfast nap. "What the hell do you want?" He opens the door. I notice the bathroom door ajar and figure Kekoa is in it.

"Rupert, I brought you a margarita. Doesn't that sound good?"

He stammers and smacks his mouth, surveying the drink. His legs pull to the floor like a rusty elevator, and he reaches for it.

I sit next to him on his bed.

"Um. Weak, don't you think? Say, why are you here? Did you stay all night?" He puts the drink down.

"No, Rupert, silly boy, I went to get you this drink. I brought a friend so he could use your bathroom and clean up. Do you want to go to lunch?"

"Yes, yes." He nods and sits, slumps, and seems to process what I said. His eyes brighten. "Okay, help me to my feet. My feet are old, you know, eighty-five. Now, my face isn't that old, no. What'd you think, say sixty?"

I see one caterpillar eyebrow raise, lifting one side of his face while the other sags, taking on the weight of gravity's handiwork over his eighty-five years. Lying isn't a sport for me. "You're old if you don't deal with God. If you receive His love and forgiveness and ask Him to be your Father, you're timeless. Heaven never ends."

"Um. I'll think about that one." He rises and takes mini steps toward the door. "Coming? I'll treat."

I smile, knowing that he knows I get free food. "No. But go ahead. I'll wash my face and be on my way." In two strides, I reach Rupert, pat him on the shoulder, and shut the door behind him. "You can come out now," I say to Kekoa in the bathroom.

Kekoa opens the door backward, so his hands can twist the knob. He stands in the opening. Mascara is under, over, and in his eyes. Lipstick is all around his mouth. The purple bags under his eyes and the way his shoulders sag make him look as if he had pulled a month's worth of twenty-four-hour shifts. He leans against the door frame for support.

"My cuffs." His shoulders do this twitchy rise and fall. He leans his head back to rest it. "Is this the end? If I jump overboard like this, the blood from my wrists will attract sharks."

Blood? "Let me see."

Kekoa walks closer and turns around. The flesh around his cuffs bleeds down into his hands. Dried blood trails down his pants.

"Oh, Kekoa." I take his fingers in mine. "This is terrible. You need medical attention."

He turns. "Are you making fun of me?"

I sit back, stunned. "No. Why would I do that? I will never make fun of you."

His head hangs. "Sorry. My brother is a drama queen. He'd totally laugh at me right now."

"I'm not him." My fingers touch his. I rise and get disinfectant soap from the bathroom and wash his wounds the best I can. "I popped up to see Stayton. He wrote on a napkin that security is watching him. He said there was no key, but there is a passcode. What's he talking about?"

Kekoa sits next to me on the bed. "Passcode. Like a password maybe."

I study the digital virtual assistant in our room, a plastic rose, and ask, "Siri, on the ship, the Golden Princess, is there a passcode for handcuffs?"

"I searched the ship for information, but there's a password needed to verify identification before I can answer that question." The rose-shaped device says, resting on a marbled dome the diameter of an orange.

Kekoa spins around. "What? Where?"

I put my hand on his back. "It's okay. You've never heard of a digital virtual assistant before?"

He stares at the rose. "No," his voice has a higher pitch than usual, and barks a laugh.

I giggle. "Siri, what's the weather for Lihue today?"

"Today in Lihue you can expect partly cloudy skies with a high of eighty-one and a low of seventy-two."

Kekoa looks at it like it's an egg ready to hatch. "What can it tell us?"

"She finds answers to your questions on the internet. People use her to set alarms to wake them up, give them information, or book appointments. You can ask her to play whatever music you want."

"Really?"

Kekoa is like a child looking through the window of a pastry shop.

"Where did you grow up that you've never seen one of these before?" I ask.

After a pause, he answers, "In our private heaven." His eyes stare as if he can see through the walls and taste heaven. Tears well in his eyes.

I can't help myself but slide close to him and slip my arms around him to pull him close. My ears hear the thu-thump, thu-thump, thu-thump of his heart. My hands caress his muscled back. If only I could find out more about this mysterious mountain man. He melts into me and then backs away. His eyes carry a thousand pounds of sorrow.

"To protect them, I had to leave my family, and I don't want to leave you too. But you're in danger if you're with me." His lips part, and he looks at my lips and into my eyes.

His eyes show an intense desire for me, not only a physical longing, but to know me.

"I have to get away." He continues. "Prison, a career military experience, homelessness. I don't know what awaits me. Don't love me. I can't give you what I want to give you." He presses his eyes closed.

"Let me help you."

Kekoa tilts his head and purses his lips. "Lily, your 'M. O.' is to rescue helpless men."

My mouth drops open. How dare he. "I . . . I don't rescue helpless men. I help drunks. There's a lot of crime going on right now."

"Tell me about your dad," he says. His voice is soft.

"What are you, a psychologist? Give me a break. I've ended my career on this ship to help you."

"Thank you," he says.

His eyes, puppy dog eyes, tell me he means it.

"Look, I don't want to put you down. I think you're an amazing, beautiful, sacred, smart, and sweet girl—woman. Mom used to be a counselor before she raised me. She taught us some things about family systems," he says.

Kekoa pulls his lips into his mouth as if his words are too painful to speak. I'm undone by his praise. No man told me those things unless he wanted something.

"Mom made my brothers and me go through this whole marriage training book," he continues, "so we could prepare ourselves for real love, not lust. She taught us to beware of using someone to fill a hole in our hearts. I don't want you to mother me because you need to be needed."

The jerk. I slap his face and step back. "I'm not mothering you."

CHAPTER FOURTEEN

Lily

Kekoa's face is red. Not just from the slap I gave him. And not the red of a sunburn. The red you get when you feel stupid and ashamed. His shoulders droop. His chin is on his chest. Tears wash mascara down his cheeks, taking some of the rose color I rubbed on him for blush. Gentle eyes rake me over the rocks of my lies.

My conscience kicks me. He's right. Kekoa isn't trying to hurt me. My voice is soft when I say, "My father was a drunk. Mom put up with him because she needed his financial support, but then he got liver cancer. I'd come home from high school and take care of him while Mom worked. I do need to be needed."

"We all do to some extent, but you don't have to be owned by it."

The air dances like live electricity as if my dress came out of the dryer and started dancing without me. Kekoa understands me. It's as if he could see me come home, unable to date or go to friends' houses. It was my job to take care of Dad. Kekoa opened a door I don't know how to go through. He sees me in my trap. I love him for it, but when I put my hand up to touch his arm, I shake. My mouth forms the words "Thank you," but no sound emerges. I can't ruin this moment. Last forever, this moment.

"You need me," I say. "You can't function outside this cabin door with your hands in shackles."

He nods. "These cuffs must come off, but I am not your responsibility. I need you, but not as someone whose job it is to take care of me but to be my brother."

"Brother?" I shake my head.

"Brother. I've never had a sister and want you to be my brother, my friend. Otherwise, I have no clue how to treat you."

He's clueless about how to treat a girl, but no guy has ever treated me with such respect. After rubbing the back of my neck, I fidget with the button at the bottom of my shirt. "I don't know how. My brother was a toddler when I left for the cruise ship. Taking care of him landed on my shoulder, too."

Kekoa smiles and turns his head to an angle. "Then I'll teach you." He sits on the corner of the bed, leans forward, and tries to stretch the best he can with his hands bound. "I have a problem. I'm in cuffs. Mom would say to brainstorm ideas, and you can help me. Together, we can think. No idea is stupid, throw out anything."

"Okay, ideas." I sit next to him, but when I examine his cuffs, there is no keyhole. "Siri, how do you open handcuffs?"

"Here's what I found out on the web. Cufflinks made before 2025 need a key to open. In the United States, Michael Boyton patented a cufflink using code-to-open in 2026, widely used in the judicial system today."

Kekoa's eyebrows raise a bit.

Rupert's reading glasses rest on the table. I put them on and examine the cuffs. I find a small copyright symbol and the year 2026. "Yes, 2026 and a number and letter combination. Now, we just need the code." I find a pen on the dresser buried under a white handkerchief and write the combination that hopefully identifies the specific handcuff.

Kekoa asks, "Siri, who is the head of security on the Golden Princess Cruise Ship?"

"The Golden Princess Cruise Ship, owned by G and G Adventure Incorporated, hired Siegfried Jacobsen in 2047. Does that answer your question?"

Kekoa stares at the device. "Yes, thank you."

The pink rose says, "You're welcome. Have a good day."

I laugh and slap Kekoa's knee.

"Siri," he asks, "is Siegfried Jacobsen who works for G and G Adventure Incorporated married?"

"According to public record, Siegfried Jacobsen is divorced."

We glance at each other and say, "Silver" at the same time.

"Siri, does Siegfried Jacobsen who works for G and G Adventure Incorporated have any children?"

"According to public record, Siegfried Jacobsen has one daughter named Melody Lehua Jacobsen. Does that answer your question?"

I'm ready to dance.

"Yes," Kekoa says and looks at my note. "Siri, what material are 2026 handcuff CH5937232 made from?"

"Model 2026 CH5937232 handcuffs are created from a plastic fourteen times stronger than the steel used for body armor, helmets, aircraft, and vehicles used in war products. It's called ultrahigh molecular weight polyethylene or UHMWPE. Was that helpful?"

Kekoa sighs a ribbon of disappointment a mile long. "Yes." He raises his head. "We can't cut it or saw it." His eyes close in what seems like a silent prayer.

He touches the paper with the code. "Siri, can you release the lock on handcuff CH5937232?"

"CH5937232 is an authorized handcuff with G and G Adventures Inc. A security code is needed for me to unlock this device."

Kekoa takes a deep breath and blows it out of his lips. "Siri, open handcuff CH5937232."

"Please tell me the security code to authorize me to open handcuff CH5937232."

"m e l o d y," he says.

"That is not the security code for this device. Would you like to try again?"

Kekoa plops down on the bed again and sits still. His eyes have dark circles under them. Everything about him droops.

I think about what my code would be if Melody were my daughter. *Please, God, tell me.* "Siri, open the handcuff we just mentioned."

"Please tell me the security code to allow me to open handcuff CH5937232," the device says.

"m e l o d y m y # 1," I say.

A clink sounds from Kekoa's wrists, and the cuffs unlock. I gasp and push Kekoa around so I can examine them. The cuffs stick to the blood on his wrists. "Oh my gosh. You're free. Just let me wash your wounds so taking the cuffs off doesn't rip your skin." I rush to the bathroom and soak a clean washcloth in hot water and clean his wrists. Once I slip them off, he pulls his arms forward and swings them around, laughing.

"Thank you. Thank you. Thank you." He pulls me off the ground in a hug and tries to swing me around, but my feet hit the bed and we both fall onto the floor. Kekoa gets up before me and gives me his hand to pull me up. "Thanks, Brother," he says.

CHAPTER FIFTEEN

Kekoa

I'm beside myself with hope the moment my shackles open. One impossible component down, fifteen more to go. My wrists are open wounds, but Lily uses Rupert's razor and rips up an extra pillowcase to make bandages. Not that they're going to last long. We need to get off this ship. To swim in salt water with open wounds will hurt, but not as much as staying in hell's lair. The bleeding stops. At least there will be no dried blood.

"Lily, I'm going to need to swim for it. I don't expect you to come. But thank you." Gazing into her eyes is like slipping into a hot tub—I never want to pull myself out. How could I have ever compared Ingrid to her?

"I'm going with you," she says.

"No. I'll be sleeping under a tree and eating fallen, forgotten fruit, half-rotted. I have no future."

"Did you do that on purpose, the fallen fruit thing?" Her face tilts in amusement.

I smile. "Sorry, I like poetry."

"Corny." An impish grin emerges from her "mother" face. "But I like it, Brother."

I stand and say, "Thank you for this," and hold out my bandaged wrists. "Will you go outside and see if Kauai is visible?"

To have a girl so close to me gives me chicken skin. Just when I start to care, and she cares back, I have to leave.

Lily leaves and returns. "Yes, I can make out land in the distance," she says.

We slip outside. Fresh salt air makes my heart sing. I don't have sea legs on a ship, but in the ocean, I'm home.

The rugged mountain ranges of Kauai silhouettes the sky. Bright white edges on puffy clouds radiate the sun's brightness behind them. Warm air welcomes me home.

Together, we sneak down the stairs. Lily looks for Security. If she doesn't find any, she will motion for me to come. Otherwise, we will turn back and wait. At last, we reach the bottom deck. I hold her in my arms and whisper,

"Thank you. A thousand times, thank you." I flip over the rail and climb straight down a giant chain toward a lifeboat secured near water level for anyone who falls over. Nawiliwili lighthouse is in view. It's about noon. The ship will enter Nawilliwilli Bay soon. Its berth takes up the entire pier within the hour. Security will expect me to jump ship once we dock. They'll be ready for me. I've seen passengers go through the narrow pathway between high fences watched by guards. To swim to the shore of my choosing is a better choice. Lily will change her mind about coming with me once she realizes she can't follow. I miss her already. My brother. But more.

When the ship reaches halfway between the lighthouse on the north side of the bay and the sea wall of rocks stretching halfway into the mouth of the bay, the ship will stop its forward movement and turn. Then I'll have the best chance of getting far enough away from the giant motors. The sucking motor that cuts everything it catches into minuscule fish food would mince me too if I am sucked into its blades.

Sounds of Lily crawling down the chain above me elicits panic in my gut. What am I getting her into? The breakwater wall lies a half mile away. To swim in the ocean is tougher than the little teal puddle passengers call their pool. Currents pull you. Waves sweep into your nose and pour water down your throat.

The motor vibrates its roar through the water and echoes off the ship's side. I'd have to yell at her to be heard and can't risk the exposure. The cabins are just on the other side of the wall.

Lifeboats are covered in white, thick tarps. That's okay. You can't see it from above, anyway. Lily's hair is streaming behind her in the wind. I pull off my shirt and pants and toss them into the ocean. The swim trunks I wear under my pants will be my only clothes but dragging a wet shirt and pants will only slow me down. Lily has shorts and her work shirt on. I circle my stiff shoulders around. My insides are a mixture of nausea, dread, and excitement. What if Lily goes for it and drowns? I swam in the ocean every day of my childhood, but I don't know if Lily has ever swum in the sea.

She kneels beside me and talks into my ear. "What now?"

"Have you ever swum in the ocean before?" My voice sounds desperate as I pull her hair aside and speak to her ear.

"I'll be fine. I can do three laps in the pool."

My heart jolts. I slap my face with my hands and point to the rocks we'll have to swim to.

"I was kidding." She punches me in the shoulder and says, "I wouldn't be here if I didn't think I could make it, Brother."

I'm not sure I can believe her and am not convinced she isn't mocking me by calling me her "brother."

It's time. The motor sounds different, turning against the tides to face the port. I dive into the sea and swim fast going up the coast, but my gut wants me to stop and make sure Lily swims fast enough to keep from getting chopped to bits.

"Go, go," she says, almost passing me.

I hope she won't wear out, but once we get away from the ship, we can roll over and tread water if we need to catch our breath.

The water's choppy. Swells take us up and down. My wrists scream in pain and the bandages float away. Water gets down my throat. I stop to cough it out and turn around to see but can't locate her. "Lily." I don't want to yell. Water carries noise, especially with the rock face on the north side of the bay to echo sounds. I turn to find her. Her arms reach out of the sea like they're worn out, facing the sea, not the shore. She must think she's following me, but the current is taking her out. I tear the water with every stroke. The wind has come up blowing against me. I must swim faster than her to catch her, and the tide is pulling her out.

I'm getting out of breath, but I can't let her drown. The waves are higher on the ocean side of the bay. Being on the bottom of the wave blocks my view. I keep on powering. *God, help us get to land. Keep Lily safe. Help her stop and look for me.*

A swell sweeps me up and down so fast I can't see her.

"Kekoa," I hear.

"Here. I'm here. Hang on. Keep calling so I can find you." I couldn't tell where the sound came from.

"Kekoa." Anguish trails in her voice.

"Don't panic. Tread water, talk." I look around. "Wave your arm." Then I see her twenty yards in front of me and swim to her.

"I can't. Where's land?" She sounds exhausted.

"Turn on your back. I'm going to pull you by your hair until you catch your breath." A valley in the tide blocks my view. In a moment, a swell takes me up and I glimpse the lighthouse. Pelts of rain torpedo down. *Lord, please make the rain stop.* With one hand hanging onto Lily's hair, I do the side stroke. I know it won't hurt her. My brothers and I used to practice "drowning" and saving each other using the techniques Mom, a former lifeguard, taught us. If only my brothers could see me saving a girl. After a few minutes, I stop. The rain has let up.

"At least we'll die together." Lily's breathing has improved. Kauai's landforms are visible, but we have made no progress toward shore, only proceeding north along the coast. We couldn't climb the cliffs on the coastline, anyway. If we swim farther, we'll come to the sandy spot I've seen when we sail around the island.

"No die. Swim close. Angle toward shore." I say through the water, messing with my words.

"K."

We swim for a long time, maybe an hour. Finally, we're close, but the coast is rocky. Having your body slammed against a rock is too likely. We breaststroke farther and find a patch of sand to land on. Once we crawl up on the sand, I laugh. As I lie on my back, she crawls over to me, and puts her head on my chest. I reach my arm around her. The tide tickles my toes, but I'm so tired I don't care. We drift off to sleep together.

I wake up. The sun flicks at my drowsiness with its rays of hope and promise. Lily is asleep, her head still on my chest, my arm under her. The tide surges in, and the foamy surf rolls up to our waist. I sit up and roll over, so I don't wake Lily. My leg plants in the soft, wet, tawny-colored sand, and I pick her up in my arms. It's hard to balance.

"Where am I?" Lily's wet hair covers her face. She sounds drunk.

"In God's country." I kiss the top of her hair and search for a place to put her. She seems to fall back asleep. A hot bath would feel good right now, a dry towel, and clothes. I chuckle; we have nothing. My wrists sting from the salt water, but I am as rich as the Facebook king who owns thousands of shoreline acres on the North Shore. Lily is in my arms. We made it off the ship.

CHAPTER SIXTEEN

Kekoa

Hale koa scrub trees with their hanging brown pods someone brought decades ago to feed the cattle line on the tiny beach's edge next to a golf course above us. We're protected for the moment from view, but I wonder what horrors I've set Lily up for, aiding a criminal. If Silver sics the law enforcement on us, it's only a matter of time before we're caught. Guinea grass fights for a place in the sand among the weeds on the unkept coastline. Large black rocks flattened by the seemingly innocuous water protrude from the surf on three sides of the little sandy beach.

I relax on a smaller black rock with rounded edges rising only a couple of feet. The rock wall holds a small patch of sand in the shape of a shamrock on the shoreline. I hold Lily as she sleeps on my lap. *What to do now?* Lily stirs.

She jumped ship with me and made it to shore. A new respect for her brims like a sunrise after a storm, like hunger after sickness.

"Kekoa." She raises her head a bit, sees the inlet, and pulls her arms around my chest and back. "We did it."

I shiver with the thrill of her arms around me. Afraid to break the spell, I hold her tight. "Thank you, God." I relax.

Lily sits up and stares up and down the coastline. "Where are we?"

"See the lighthouse? We're just north of Nawilliwilli Bay. Above us looms an enormous golf course and resort. We can walk down after five o'clock when the cruise ship pulls out. Right now, someone might recognize us. There will be hundreds of the ship's passengers swimming, shopping, and eating at Kalapaki across from where the ship sits docked."

"You know this beach?"

"Yeah. My brothers and I cruised the beaches a lot and checked out different spots. We've been to this tiny bay. That's why I chose it. Except for Nawiliwili Bay, there aren't any other sandy beaches for miles. It's rocky. Security would find us easier if we swam inside the bay."

"You haven't told me about your brothers yet."

"I will. First, let's take a shower."

"A shower?"

"Yup, follow me." I lead her up a trail to the edge of the golf course. We pass a sign informing tourists that the currents are dangerous.

"Yeah, no kidding," Lily says, reading the sign, her hands on her hips. "Wow." She takes in the lighthouse and waves that blitz the rocks below. A few clouds two-step it across the sky, and the breeze whips up her hair.

I stand behind her and pull her backward a step, putting my arms around her. She puts her hands on top of mine, and we breathe in the belt of beauty as far as the eye can see in both directions.

To the left of the path, an eight-foot black stone wall with two showerheads tucks under banana trees next to a covered picnic table. I walk around them, but all the bunches of bananas are too green to eat. My mouth is dry. We shower and drink. They do not heat the water like on the cruise ship, but it's not cold. To dry off and get warm, we sit on the perfect carpet—golf course grass.

The rich, green turf reminds me of the solid colors in a child's picture book. The green has hills, valleys, and divots of tan sand traps. I've heard tourists comment colors are brighter on Kauai than on the mainland, but I've never been to the continental U.S. to know.

Lily says, "You have to tell me why security is gunning for you." Concern drips from her eyes.

I trust her and tell her about my family and how I ended up on the ocean liner.

She asks about Ingrid. "Why did she ask you to go to dinner after being so distant?"

"I don't know. Maybe it's a woman thing. But she kept my drinking glass as a souvenir—I think. Then she wanted me to swim, showed me the lost and found, and I got these swim trunks. I wore them all the time under my uniform to keep from leaving them."

Lily stares off. Her brows twists in puzzlement. "I wonder if she was trying to determine your DNA by keeping your glass. She could plant evidence and blame you for something she did because you're a Neverborn."

"I wish I could use my DNA to track down my birth mother and father."

"You can."

"What? No. I can't buy or sell, remember? If I do, they'll trace 'Clint.' And besides, I doubt there's any money in Clint's account."

"But I can. Is there a drugstore near?"

"You can? How?"

"A saliva kit will do it. We'll send it in and wait for the results to be posted online. I did it for a friend not too long ago. But first, let's find something to eat. I'm so hungry."

We walk several miles, past the golf course, to Lihue Pasta. I pull my wet tip money out of the zipped compartment in my trunks and ask if they take cash. We use cash so our transactions aren't traceable. The server laughs and says, "Not normally, but I'll make an exception in your case." He eyes Lily. Her hair needs brushing; it looks sexy and kind of messy. It's Hawaii, eating after being in the sea is normal. A resentment toward him burns in my chest. I want to say, "She's mine." But he walks off to place our order.

Lily eats shrimp scampi, and I scarf their steak special. I could have eaten six of them.

Then we saunter down the road and buy Lily a tropical dress and slippers for both of us. She wants me to buy a matching shirt, but when would I wear a shirt? I compromise and buy a cheap t-shirt.

My palms sweat, and I walk on puffy pink clouds going to the drugstore. Anticipation squirts delight through me even more than eating Mom's sweet potato fry bread. I might find out who my birthmother is. I keep walking too fast for Lily.

"Slow down, Dude." She holds me back by clasping my hand. I've never walked with a girl before. Her legs are shorter—she takes smaller steps.

We put the test, a hairbrush, shampoo, and hair conditioner in the red cart in the store.

She slips a small box into the cart surreptitiously.

"What are those?" I pick up the package and study the picture.

She turns and walks away.

I follow her. "Did I do something wrong?" But she keeps walking away. It's a package of tampons. Mom taught me about women's menstrual cycles, but a woman having a period is a distance fact in my brain, not a reality. I'm lower than dust on the cement floor. The package slips from my hand into the cart. I've embarrassed her. My ears burn off my head from the heat, and I hit my forehead with my palm and moan.

After surveying the chocolate aisle, I pick up a chocolate rose. I pay for the items and find her. She's pretending to look at make-up.

"You don't need any make-up," I say.

"Any?" She pretends not to be embarrassed, trying to act nonchalant.

"Make-up. You're perfect without any." I hand her the sack.

Her fingers reach out for it and touch my hand. Like a treasure frozen in time, the warmth of her fingertips lingers. She notices the rose in the bag, and smiles. "Thank you. I'll be right back." She disappears into the bathroom.

When she comes out and we go outside into the sunlight, her long hair shines, chestnut with tinges of red in it and brushed. She glues her eyes to mine. "Hi, I don't think we've met. I'm Lily." She extends her hand.

I smile. Her eyes are bigger, browner than I remember, like a world inviting me in.

We walk to the post office. "Does it hurt? Your period?" My voice wavers.

"Sometimes I have cramps when my period first starts. All that swimming yesterday washed away my bloating. I'm more tired and cranky. So, watch out, Bub," she says and looks at me with laughter in her eyes.

"I'll be on my best behavior. We don't want any cranky outbreaks on my first date with a beautiful girl."

"First date, huh? What about Ingrid?"

"She was glamorous, not beautiful. There's a difference. I like beautiful."

We walk hand in hand and talk about what we see in the stores that we like or what we want our first home to look like. I can ask my thousand questions to a real girl. It's hard to remember I'm a wanted man, and that Silver could have seen security camera footage of Lily taking Ingrid's badge. Someone would then suspect her of collaborating with Ingrid's murderer. I shouldn't be so happy.

Waiting in line at the post office seems so normal. I did it scores of times, mailing packages for Mom and Dad to their other kids and grandkids. A longing to see my parents wraps me like paper on a present. I can't wait for them to meet Lily and tell them about the ship. But I can't see them or do anything that would lead the authorities to arrest and prosecute them for kidnapping. *Please, Lord, let them not worry about me.* They must feel sick with concern and sadness at my disappearance. I sure need prayer. *Lord, vindicate us; free us, and show us what to do.*

CHAPTER SEVENTEEN

Kekoa

It will take the Honolulu DNA agency a day to process the DNA results and put the saliva sample data into the computer. A day. A night. Whoa. Where should we stay? Resorts and hotels require identification, and it's already afternoon.

"What next?" Lily looks at the greeting cards next to the line, waiting for postal workers to process their packages.

"Let's go to a thrift store and buy pillows, blankets, and anything else that we want."

"Okay." She glances at the people in the post office and loses her smile as if she's afraid someone there might call the police on us.

We send our package unhindered and walk to the Salvation Army's thrift store. The bedding and clothes for

Lily are decent and cheap. Our last stop is Pizza Plus, to grab a pizza for dinner.

There's a run-down tiny house west of Nawiliwili Bay where my folks used to store their tables and chairs for the market. We can sleep there. But passing by the major arteries of roads and sidewalks to reach it would leave us dangerously exposed. Lily chats about her best friend, Amanda, and the adventures they created in high school, but I can't concentrate. There are only three routes that cross over the Kukui Mall area of Lihue. To trek out close to the bay is out of the question, but taking either of the two other routes would leave us visible. I choose the Haleko Road route. It's the closest.

Flying cars hover above the road in the public lanes for PlanePods. Even so, the street has a steady stream of the electric rental cars tourists love. Most light up their cars in a teal exterior, with holograms of waves breaking in the ocean. Others choose fire or ice, or a solid color to illuminate. "Aloha" seems their favorite greeting to post on their back windshield, although some flash, "Thank you" when someone lets them in. An orange Mustang copy convertible passes us going down the ravine where the banana poka swirls up the forest it kills. The viny weed chokes trees with its frosting of green leaves and lavender flowers. A convertible Mustang jerks over, and Silver yells, "Get them!" to the security guy next to him.

I pull Lily's hand and then drop it as we jump the guardrail and run into the dense underbrush. Praying as I go, my brain goes from peace to pure adrenaline. We'll get caught fighting vines if we stay in this maze.

Lily grabs the back of my shorts to keep up with me. I head back toward the post office, but I realize Silver might call for more of his cronies. Some might wait on Rice Street by the post office, the east side, and some on the west side by the car dealership. I need to catch my breath and hide inside the green carpet of vines with the spiders, but we keep moving through the vines huffing. We reach the edge of a dumpy shack and the remnants of a stream. I hear Silver's voice yelling in the distance, "Kekoa, there's a warrant out for your arrest. Stop, otherwise, we can't help and defend you."

Warrant out for my capture? Why? To cover *your* crimes. I stop, and we run across the yard and over a wire fence, rusty and misshapen. We wind up the gully and end up on a thread of a street. It winds up to Rice Street. We climb a tree at the back of a gas station lot on Rice Street.

Lily stays right behind me. Once I'm satisfied that we're well hidden, I sit on a limb panting. She perches on another next to me. We can't see out, which means nobody can see in.

"Does security have heat sensors?" Lily says, still breathing hard.

"Heat sensors?"

"Yeah. Police use them to find fugitives. I think that applies to us right now."

I adjust my feet as I stand on a lower branch and grasp a bough with my hand, so the limb doesn't jab into my butt. "Why? Ingrid cleared me of the petty room thefts. Do they think I killed her?"

"Ingrid cleared you?"

"Yeah, before she asked me to go swimming in the staff pool."

"Why would she do that? Grab your glass, clear you of theft charges, take your picture, and then ignore you and disappear?"

We look at each other.

Lily unzips a pocket in her shorts and pulls out her phone, wrapped in a sealed plastic bag.

"Nice," I say.

"At least I didn't drop it in the vines." She touches it, and it springs to life. "We'll need it to check."

Her eyes narrow and intently focus. She googles the results of my DNA test, but they're not posted yet. The mail might not reach Honolulu until tomorrow. She searches for the local news using "cruise ship" in the search bar. An article appears, "Cruise Ship Murder Involves Local Police." She reads the synopsis of the article about an unnamed security employee found in her cabin dead.

"Assuming Ingrid was murdered, why?" An ambulance whizzes past Rice Street. Lily studies me.

A chill shakes me. Murdered. Ingrid. I never talked to her about God, and it's too late now.

"She was a snake. Sorry to say it. It could be a jealous lover, a vengeful victim of her thefts, a drug dealer, anyone," Lily says.

How could I have been so taken with her? Why did I trust so easily? First, Clint talks me into leaving, and I think he's offering me a job because he's just looking for a vacation on the island. Then I think Ingrid likes me.

I hear dogs barking, and I know that police have dogs that have followed fugitives that have broken out of jail in the past. Lily would have left clothes on the ship with her scent on them. "We have to get out of here," I say and start down the tree.

A gray-haired man gasses up an older car. I approach him, Lily behind me, "Hey, which way are you going? Can I pay you to drop us off at a store?"

He considers me and puts the handle back on the pump lever. "I'm going by Safeway. You two can jump in the back."

"Great." We hop in his Camry and pass Silver's car going down Rice Street toward the bay. Lily and I catch each other's eyes.

I offer the driver twenty dollars when we arrive.

He pockets it and takes off.

We work our way through the driveway toward the residential area next to it. "Thanks," I say to him and wave.

We left the pizza somewhere in the banana poka, but hiding takes priority over buying more food. At least we got to the other side of Lihue, but we'll still have to walk on the main roads to get to the beater house. Lily pulls her phone out of her bra where she stashed it to have her hands free.

We watch and listen for Silver's car trekking through the neighborhood. The streets have newer houses on them, multimillion dollar homes. Houses are so expensive in Hawaii. There are multiple cars in front of each home. Often, extended family members live together to save money. Only the rich can afford to buy a house.

Children ride their hoverboards along the sidewalk. Every house roof is solar. Most yards have solar stations for their cars, boat motors, and toys. We cut across a golf course to stay off the roads. Hover golf carts dart through the grass. Some duffer wears an Irish cap and yells at us.

"Run," I say. Once on the main street, Nawiliwili Road, we catch our breath and loop through neighborhoods even if it's farther. At least, it's less visible than the main highway down toward the bay. Sweat marks my shirt. I wish we'd at least found and filled some water bottles.

We're forced to walk on the main road once the residential area ends. Running might seem suspicious, so we walk fast. Finally, a sideroad up to the enormous storage unit takes us where we want to go. Winding down the minor road and then into a small neighborhood, we trek on to the house. It's the size of a large shed. I pick up a couple of water bottles thrown onto the grass, and we go to the Small Boat Harbor, clean the bottles, and fill them. The cruise ship looms in the distance above all the peon boats in the harbor. A heaviness presses down on me, remembering the confines of the ship and Silver's oppression. I wish I could shake it off and say it's over, but it's not. They have issued a warrant for my arrest. Did Silver kill Ingrid?

Menehune Fishpond lies upriver, along a bend of the Hule'ia River. It's a lake with just a ribbon of land between it and the river flowing on the south side. We hike to it. I ache for a fishing line to catch fish for dinner.

Today is Thursday. Mom and Dad will cruise into the bay early Saturday morning with my brothers for the market. If only it were today. I want to cry.

"You okay?" Lily puts her arm on my back.

I man up and swallow. "Yeah. I'm just thinking about my family coming to sell on Saturday. I don't dare go see them lest someone connect them with me. We could benefit from their food and advice, and Dad would know what to do."

Lily stands in front of me. "I can go see them."

I grin and kiss the top of her head. "Great idea."

We stumble onto a mountain apple tree in the woods on the way back to the wreck of a house.

"Apples?" Lily says.

"Mountain apples," I say and take off my shirt to create a bag so we can carry them back.

She bites into one. "Hm. They don't taste like apples, more like plums, but they sure look like little red apples. They're sweet."

We look homeless as we carry our fruit and water bottles to the tin-roofed decrepit sugar plantation shack. Rain blew in from holes in the wall, so Uncle found a storage unit to rent instead. The shed is empty and decomposing. I remember the combination to open the lock, his birthday. At one time someone painted dark green on the outside with white trim. Now, the whispers of the original green blend with the ironwood tree, haole koa, and Guinea grass all trying to enclose the cottage. Lily brushes off the counter by the sink in the larger room. There's a tiny room with a broken-out window adjoining it.

In the woods, I find a trashed area where some homeless person once lived. Rope, a tin can, and a lighter lay among the debris. When I return, Lily is sweeping with an ironwood tree limb.

"That's resourceful," I say.

"Yeah? What'd you find?"

"Rope. For your hammock."

She watches as I weave branches with the rope to form a crude hammock tied to a hook in the kitchen and the broken window frame on the other side of the room. I can sleep on the floor, but she's not going to. I find a noni tree and collect the large leaves. By weaving them like Kana, I make two mats. One for Lily to lie on and one she can cover herself with since we dropped our bedding and clothes somewhere in the banana poka forest. Toward morning, the air chills.

Lily looks cute curled in her hammock, her hair draping down like silken seaweed, swirling with the sway. I sit in the corner and watch her, in awe of her beauty. How complete I feel around her—a cool breeze to my sweaty body, sweet mango to my constant craving.

Will all this end? When she goes to my family's market stand, will she fall for my golden brother Canyon and leave me behind like a fish who lays eggs and then swims off?

Tomorrow, I could find out my birth parent's identity. Or the cops might arrest me for murder.

CHAPTER EIGHTEEN

Kekoa

Man, I'm hungry. I glance over and see Lily sleeping though the sun is up. There aren't any papaya trees around to harvest for breakfast. I trek down toward Menehune Fishpond and then back to the homeless trash heap where I'd found the rope looking for anything I could use to catch or net fish. A cigarette lighter hides between two rocks with a piece of wood on it forming a stool. Vegetable package netting swirls in a heap of paper bags half decomposed in the grass. I create a fishnet by weaving a bent branch through it. At the fishpond, it nets a couple of fish.

I step into the shed with my fish rather proud of myself.

"Where have you been?" Lily's voice sounds feathered with panic.

"Oh, Lily. I'm sorry. I didn't think you'd miss me. You were sleeping." The fish drop from my hands. I never knew a voice could cut me deeper than a razor blade.

The cold fish hit her feet, and she screams. "I thought—"

She bursts into tears.

I pull her into my arms with one hand behind her head and the other behind her back. She sobs in my arms. All for the sake of breakfast, I bring all this despair. If she gets cranky and tired during her period, maybe she gets emotional, too.

Lily lets out a somber, shaking sob and collects herself. "I thought Silver found you."

"Oh, Sweetie." I meant to say, "sweet Lily." But she smiles and holds me tight. Mom would wish me to affirm her in the way she made each of us do with our brothers when we were hurting. "You must have been terrified that something happened to me. I left you alone, unprotected, and abandoned. Is that it?"

Her arms go slack for a moment. She pulls back and wipes her tears with her finger and studies my eyes. "Yes. Yes. Yes." She hugs me hard. "I was so afraid I'd never see you again." She pushes her forehead into my chest bone. "That you were headed to some awful prison for someone else's crime." Her voice changes to a pleading one. "God, please don't let that happen. Please free us from Silver's grip."

I hold her and feel her relax and rest against me. I've come home. A home not made of wood or rock, but understanding and acceptance.

After adjusting her feet, she looks down and sees the fish in the net.

"Ew," she says and jumps back.

I hold them up. "Fish for breakfast."

Lily covers her head with her hands. "I'm sorry. My foot touched the cold fish, and I freaked."

"Yes, you did." I laugh. Stress rolls off me like scales, and I reach for her again.

After some minutes, Lily says, "Oh, let me charge my phone and see if we have gotten any DNA results yet."

I release her and she takes her phone outside and sets it to the solar charge. It's nearly a cloudless day. She sets it on a leaf in the sun. "I'm starving. How do we eat fish without a stove?"

My guerilla side wants to jump up and down and yell, "I know. Let me do it," but I pretend to be cool and say, "I'll build a fire and serve your entrée in a moment, Ma'am."

With big rocks to place by the shed, my "stove" comes to life. Dry brush and kukui nuts create a base to light them with the cigarette lighter I'd found. The flame licks up the dried brush quickly. Bigger wood brings the flame into a crackling fire. Then I bend over one side of a tin can lid so I don't cut myself and clean the fish. Skewered across the rocks with green sticks, the fish roast in the coals.

"Look at those nuts burn." Lily ruffles my hair as I squat over the fire.

"The ancient Hawaiians called them candlenuts. Once roasted, one would burn for their candle for forty-five minutes."

She squats next to me. "How do you know so much?"

"Six well-educated parents each taught what they'd learned to all us boys. Plus, we took online classes and preset coursework. No cell phones, media games, rarely movies. We played with each other in the ocean, stream, or riding down our zipline."

"You have a zipline?"

I nod. "Canyon's dad built one from the top of the ridge, zig zagging over the stream from one side to the other. It's a blast. I hope I can take you to ride on it soon."

Her face shines like Cinderella opening the door to the prince carrying her shoe. "I can't wait to meet these people." Her phone beeps, and Lily picks up her phone to check it. "I got it. Oh my gosh. Get a pencil. Get a pencil.

I put my hands up. *There are no pencils here.*

"Birth mother is Maili Leilani Kaaumoana. Birth father is Damian Vaskier."

She chats about their names, talking faster than I can follow. Her brain seems to speed up to that of our zipline flying down the canyon. My brain seems stuck on "birthmother." Before, she was a concept, the abortion participant. Now, I realize she's a person. With a name. A story. A soul. Indignation swells in me. I wish I could say when you think you have the right to your own body, you forget I have my own body. My body may be inside yours because God made you to protect me, but I have my own brain. Heartbeat. Fingers. Feelings.

Lily realizes I haven't written it down. She taps her phone to find the addresses of both. I sit on the floor of the shed's warped brown door and see where the subfloor has rotted out.

"Your birth father lives in Los Angeles. He's. What? He's the CEO of Excelsior Technology. Kekoa, your father's rich. And powerful." She's practically dancing around the fish fire.

My heart sinks with a lead weight. Maili, my birthmother, has a Hawaiian name, while my birth father is Hispanic and rich. Was the love of the good life more important to them than their child? I'm delighted to hear her story and want to understand her. On the other hand, I long to go back to my canyon and forget I ever listened to these words—like a mermaid who couldn't breathe in the water or walk on land. I wasn't born or wanted, and my very breath puts my actual family in danger.

Lily just stares at me. "What's wrong? I thought you'd be thrilled."

"Opening this door could uncover a centipede's nest. They might crawl out by the hundreds to sting me and crawl up my pants." I plant my face in my palms, my elbows on my knees. Turmoil, a cauldron of poison, simmers in my gut.

Lily puts her hand on my head. She says nothing. I see her eyes close. She's praying for me.

"How can I do this? I'm a screwup. I even screwed up being born," I say.

"Was it your fault your mother didn't want you?"

"Maybe I wasn't cute enough."

"Kekoa, she didn't even see you. She made that decision before you were born. You owe it to her to listen to the real story, not your conjecture." She plays with my hair. "And you're more than cute. You're deliriously handsome."

My head juts out at her last comment. Deliriously handsome? What does that mean? Her touch feels so soothing. Mom used to say I was her cuddle bug. Touching is my love language. Lily's right, of course, about needing to not judge Maili. I have to meet her to beg her to give me a birth certificate, but also to hear her story. An ache hits my gut. What will she say?

Lily memorizes Maili's address in Poipu. We hitchhike most of the way, and then, as Lily's phone directs us, we walk the rest.

The small house has a balcony on the second floor with an ocean view, though it's in a residential area a half mile from the beach, and a mile east of Brennecke's Beach where the lifeguards patrol the main swimming area. It's around twenty years old, painted beige with brown trim around the windows, hiding the red dirt that blows on the south shore, no doubt. They have newer solar roofing. A white, clean Tesla sits in the driveway under the house. Concrete bricks hold up the sides and foundation. Lily bounces up the stairs in front of me while I plod behind. She circles her fingers to motion for me to hurry.

She knocks the moment I get to the top before I can back out.

CHAPTER NINETEEN

Kekoa

My birthmother—a tall Hawaiian-looking woman with kinky long black hair wearing shorts and a tight-fitting tube top over her ample figure, opens the door. Her earphone must be turned on. She's conversing. "Hey, I gotta go. Someone's at. . ." After looking at me, she whispers in a wooden voice, "End call." As she bends forward at the waist, the woman's chest heaves. Her eyes are wide and deep set, glued to me. She says, "Noooooo."

A mid-teen approaches her. "What, Mom?"

They both stare at me with jaws as open as a feeding whale.

Lily jumps in. "Maili, this is your son, Kekoa."

Maili screams. "No! This isn't happening." She slams the door, but we can hear their conversation from outside.

"Mom, he's like my twin. Who is he?" We look at each other with an expression of amusement, not sure what to do next.

The boy opens the door again, and we see Maili's dumbfounded face. She slumps. Her hand covers her mouth as she stares at me. The boy says, "Hi, who are you, and why do you look like me?"

Lily jumps in since I'm standing dumb as a rock. "Kekoa is your brother, or at least your half-brother. We just got the DNA test back, see?" She shows the boy the test result.

The teen swears and holds the cellphone out for his mom to read. "Mom, he's your son too; check this out. You never told me I had a brother." The boy and I stare at each other for a long moment.

Maili shakes as she leans against the wall beside her. Under her breath, she mumbles, "Damian is gonna kill me— or you." She looks at me as if tigers in her heart claw at her, gnawing at her hopes and dreams, condemning her, and burying her hopes. Only at that moment do I forgive her. I see the demons inside. How unlike my actual mother—the wrinkled gray lady who cuddled me, believed in me, and cherished me all my life. This shell of a mother props up herself any way she can—a tent about to fall unless she finds some kind of spear to hoist and fasten to her flimsy fabric of life. Her stake must be Damian.

"Maili, this will come as a shock. I survived the abortion." My voice breaks. I can't tell her about my canyon or my family. She's not trustworthy.

She blinks like she wants to shut out what I've just said.

The boy's face freezes. "Mom, you had an abortion?"

Maili stares blankly, and she slides to the floor; her shoulders and palms are slack.

"Mom, is he Damian's son too? Mom?" Utter dismay bleeds from his voice. I resonate with the panorama of emotions I detect in his voice. Disillusionment. Shock. Confusion. Hope?

Neighbors walking their dogs pass by and stare at us in this upscale neighborhood. The boy, my look-a-like brother, says, "Come in; we don't want the entire neighborhood to gossip about us."

We walk in and see my birth mother on the floor in her own wretchedness. Lily kneels next to her, speaking in a voice as gentle as a harp, "Maili, we didn't come to judge you. It must have been hard making that decision."

I want to kiss Lily for her tenderness as she talks to Maili.

She looks up at Lily with a whisper of hope. "Can you help me up? I need to change."

Lily helps her stand, and I see the wet place on the floors and the back of her pants reveal how traumatic this is for her.

"I'm Makani," my brother says, reaching out his taupe hand. Admiration fills his eyes. He has brown, almond-shaped eyes similar to mine. His nose is straight and well-shaped. Even his lips are like mine—and Maili's. Will her pink lips speak the truth—or lies?

She trudges off, embarrassed and overwhelmed, no doubt.

I reach for Makani and give him a bear hug. He laughs as if he's always wanted a big brother. Pushing his shoulders back, I ruffle his wavy black hair the way Dad would tousle mine. "Good-looking guy!"

"Like you. Come in, and I'll get you something to drink if you want." Makani leads us to the couch.

There's a high ceiling with a giant mahogany paddle fan of carved palm fronds. The room is clean with a tan linen sectional couch on one side and two recliner chairs on the other. The tables are all made of koa or mahogany wood etched with palm frond and plumeria designs. There's the glass ocean view wall and to the right, a solid theater wall.

The two recliners face it. The other side has a large oil painting of the Kilauea lighthouse.

"Sure. I'll take whatever you have."

"Is Damian your dad too?" Makani asks and pulls out SoBes for Lily and me.

"Yes, he is, but he doesn't know about me yet." I admire this boy, my new brother.

"Me neither. Mom sends me away every time he comes to Kauai, twice a year—for two weeks. I have to live with my grandma. My father, the one with other kids he lives with and supports, doesn't even know I exist."

The fire of bitterness burns the edges of his voice. That vacuum must fill his very existence.

As I follow him by the door on the northwest side of the floor, I pick up Maili's voice in the next room. "Damian, what do I do?" I want to wait and listen, but I have to pay attention to Makani. I sip the drink and follow him into the kitchen.

Maili comes out of the bedroom a different woman. She stands tall with narrow shrewd eyes. "Makani, hele to your room until I come to get you."

Makani puts his drink on the black granite countertop. He looks from me to her and says, "No. This is my brother.

You're not going to take him away from me the way you did my dad."

She puckers her lips and flares her nostrils. Her words fire out, "Makani, go to your room, now!" As she breathes in, her breath quivers, a riverbank brimming, hovering at the edge of farmland it's reluctant to devour.

My brother's eyes tear. "What did you do, call Dad? Is that why I must hide? Is that why I have to not exist? Now Kekoa exists too. What's Dad going to do, kill him?"

Maili visibly twitches. She stretches up so tall I check to see if she is standing on her toes. She leans forward slightly and says to Makani. "I love you. I chose you. Now get to your room!" Her voice blends its plea with a desperate yell.

Lily steps forward. "We came in peace."

"Shut up!" Maili yells.

Makani slaps the granite countertop on the edge of the kitchen with his hand. "You killed him once. Dad had to be a part of that. Are you really going to kill him again? Are you going to kill me too, because I exist?"

Maili screams louder, high-pitched, "Shut up!" A string of swear words flies out of her mouth like knives. "I, I didn't kill anyone. I'm not a murderer. I'm a mother."

Lily opens her mouth to speak.

"Shut up!" Both Makani and our mom say in unison. The air is a lightning bolt storm ready to ignite a dry forest into flames.

I walk over to Makani and put my hand on his shoulder. He needs love so badly. "Makani, I want you to be my brother. Will you do that?"

Makani bursts into tears and buries his face in my chest. I hold him the way Dad held me so many times. Tears brim in my eyes, and I let them come.

I ask, "You've felt unworthy because you can't have a relationship with Damian?"

Through sobs, he says, "Yes, like if he even knew I existed, he'd be ashamed of me. I have to live invisibly as if I don't exist. Mom makes me hide."

I nod my head. "You feel invisible because your mom hides you instead of being proud of you and showing you off."

"Don't leave me. You're the only one in the whole world that understands me." Makani squeezes me tight.

Maili bows her head and in a defeated voice says, "Take Kekoa and hide! Damian's thugs are on their way. Go!"

She goes to the kitchen and pulls out a full bottle of wine. "Use this and smash the window in your room so it looks like Kekoa got away." Maili turns to Lily, "You—just disappear."

Lily looks at me. No, she looks *to* me to give her direction; she knows I care about her.

I put my hands on her shoulders and whisper, "Meet me at the surf shop at the Waiohai beach in two hours."

She nods, flies down the stairs and runs toward the beach.

I only hope I can meet her at the Waiohai in two hours.

CHAPTER TWENTY

Kekoa

Makani says, "Follow me." He runs down the outside stairs and jogs to the rear of the carport. We have no idea how much time we have before the killers are after us. After opening the door to a shelved room with ocean gear scattered, he pushes a remote. A side wall opens, and we enter his bedroom. It has a single bed, unmade, and a desk with a computer and a motley array of magazines my folks would never let me peruse. He flips up his bed into the wall, takes the bottle, and crashes the window with it. Both the window and the wine break, and dark red wine pours everywhere. He moans at the mess he'll have to clean up later.

If Damian is sending men to capture me and maybe Makani too, we'd best both disappear quickly. I hear the Holy Spirit telling me to climb and listen. "Come on, we gotta split." I pop outside to scope out the area. Makani follows. The neighbor has a mango tree expanding through most of his yard. I turn to Makani. "You own any green shirts?"

His brows pucker, "Yeah."

"Go get two."

He darts back and returns with two identical green t-shirts with a soccer team logo on them. We change, and I tie his old t-shirt to a dog slopping smiles around the neighborhood. The mutt wants to lick my face. We run to the mango tree and climb high on branches close to Maili's house.

Makani and I perch on branches next to each other. The mango stems hold small, unripe fruit hanging down like an ornament on a Christmas tree, but the foliage is dense. Breezes from the ocean make the limbs rustle. I fold a leaf and feel its smooth texture. It smells like turpentine. Makani and I glance at each other. Questions I want to ask him fill my brain. He must have as many to ask me, but now is not the time.

The increasing loud buzz comes from a couple of men approaching Maili's house in an PlanePod. They lower to the grass in the front yard. As they get out, a man with a bass voice says in a gruff tone, "This is it. I've been here before. She's Damian's mistress and the property manager of his

Kauai properties, but we're not supposed to know about the mistress' part."

"Look, a broken window." The other one cranks his neck to the left and walks over to the hidden room behind the carport. "The kid's probably not here." He stoops down and fingers the inside of the broken bottle and smells it. "Wine, what a waste."

A man's tenor voice says, "Okay, let me just blitz through the house. Then you can turn on the scent finder device and track the boy based on the odor of the dirty clothes in his bedroom."

The voices became unintelligible and more distant. The men slap up the stairs and knock. Maili lets them in, and soon they pad down to the carport and find the secret bedroom. The tenor-voiced man says, "Okay, I'll track the scent. You fly to the boy's grandma's house. Remember what Damian said, Tell Grandma that we're taking Kekoa boating. And wear your disguise."

The gravel voice laughs, "Yeah, here sharky, sharky. Why rent a boat, just bag him, and throw him off the pier?"

"We will. A million bucks for throwing garbage in the ocean. Not bad. Text me your progress."

They stop talking, so I move a branch to see better. One studies his cell phone walking in the direction of the stray dog, and the other gets in the PlanePod flying off the opposite way.

"How did you know to hang my shirt on the stupid dog?" Makani asks.

"I figured dogs might be called on to sniff us out. Who figured apps on your phone can smell?"

"But why did you put my shirt on the dog instead of yours?" Makani climbs down, swings on a branch, and drops to the ground.

"Because our mom kept you a secret, the thugs would think the bedroom was mine, not yours. The only scent they can find would have to come from your bedroom."

"How'd you get so smart?" Makani says.

"I never thought of myself as smart." Kana is smart; I've always compared myself to him and couldn't compete. "Makani, if the guy chasing the dog catches it, he's going to come back here and trace us. Follow me."

I climb to a limb hanging over the roof of a house on the street behind Maili's and scamper onto the roof, careful not to break any of the solar tiles. Makani follows me, but when I jump to a papaya tree, he grabs the limb, not the trunk. The limb breaks, but I grab his arm and press him into the trunk. Then we hop onto a roof and lower down to a tall rock wall. We walk the length. I get down to the sidewalk. "Makani, ride on my shoulders." Then I think—bikes. "Do you and your mom own bikes?"

He sits on the rock wall. "Not decent ones, just old ten-speed power bikes."

I laugh at him for not thinking they're decent. "Are they locked up?"

"They're in the back of the garage, hanging on hooks from the ceiling."

I put my hand on his knee. "Let's go get your bikes."

"Oh, yeah," he says.

Retracing our steps, we sneak into the garage, scout the neighborhood, and lift down two bikes. We hear sobs upstairs. Makani wears a mask of anger on his face, perhaps a shield from his lifetime of overwhelming emotions emanating from his mother.

"Where can we go that Damian won't expect us?" I ask him.

He thinks, "How about cane trails?"

I nod. "Good answer."

We ride north, away from Grandma's house where a thug could return from. The road weaves around like it follows a jagged coastline, not acting like a straight street. Then we twist around potholes in the old sugarcane trails, now used only by flying PlanePods relishing unpopulated space to speed. Guinea grass has multiplied like the wild chickens in these empty fields. Alerted by the sun's dip in the sky, I stop and glance at Makani's phone. I am to meet Lily in another hour. "Can Damian's thugs track you through that?"

"I don't know," he says.

His phone rings, and we look at each other. "Hello," he says.

CHAPTER TWENTY-ONE

Kekoa

A flying car swoops overhead as we pump our bikes toward Koa Lane, on the way to Maili's rented condo. I follow Makani to make sure he gets there and turn onto Poipu Road, since the back roads don't go through. The traffic is heavy with loads of tourists. Makani pumps his feet, burning off anger, but he rides recklessly. The only way he'd go to the condo was if I went with him.

"Makani, be careful; you pulled out right in front of that Honda."

"Who cares if a car smacks me? I hate my life!" he yells back. "I'm so sick of being hidden. I'd like to hide my father—under a train wreck."

By the time we reach the condo and check around for thugs, the boy is ready to tear his bike apart with his clenched fingers. He dismounts and then picks up and throws the bike against the ground.

Since the front door is open a crack, he pushes it wide and stomps in. I stand outside, listening for a minute, unsure of what to do.

"Makani, you made it, my baby." Maili says.

"I'm not *your* baby. This is xxxxed up. I'm going to kill myself the way you killed Kekoa! How would you like that?" Makani says.

His voice can be heard from across the street, poor guy.

"Don't you talk to me that way! I'm your mother."

He makes a banging sound and says, "What kind of mother kills her children before they are born?"

"I didn't kill you!" she screams. "And I didn't want to abort your brother." She bursts into tears. "I, I, I waited until the last minute and begged Damian. I wanted our child. Our baby came from Damian and me. I needed to hold him. Part of me has been crying ever since." She cries desolate sounds, the way a dog cries at his master's bed when his master has died. "I have nightmares of a baby wailing, and I wake up with a wet pillow. I hated myself, but what could I do?"

"And so, you caved—you always cave," he says with contempt in his voice. His face is red with fury.

"Stop it!" She shakes.

I'm sure people across the street can hear her scream.

"Just stop it." Her crying muffles as if she's buried her face in a pillow. "What else could I do?"

"Well, most women go on welfare and dump the jerk," Makani says in a flat tone.

My brother seems affected by her sorrow. Maybe she's acted out her grief and shame all his life.

"He would have dumped me and left me with no house and no income. Blaire, his father-in-law, is in his eighties. Damian set himself up to become the billionaire Blaire is now. If I stay, I'll have it made for the rest of my life—we'll have it made."

"You disgust me. Don't you get it? He doesn't love you. He's never loved you. He uses you. And you use him. You killed your baby because he told you to."

"No. It's *my* life and *my* body. It's *not* a baby *unless it's born*!" she shouts.

"Tell that to Kekoa, the ghost of the past who came to haunt you."

"I love Damian." Her voice comes out shrill, echoes off the walls, and reminds me of a screeching bird caught in a trap.

"Well, you've made your choice. You're not *my* mother anymore. I'm going to live with Kekoa!" A slamming sound echoes.

She yells, "You may *not* see Kekoa ever again. That boy doesn't exist. Do you hear me?"

I chuckle. He doesn't exist, huh?

"In your dreams, Mom." Makani brushes past my shoulder on the lanai and slams the door behind him. He picks up his bike lying sideways on the lawn and starts down the street. "I wish I was dead!"

I hide beside the house as she races out to the rail of the lanai.

"Makani," she wails after him, despair filling her voice. She watches him go and moans deep, soulful sounds.

When she goes in again, I ride off in the opposite direction. Lily awaits me. We had wild mood swings with Canyon's dramatic tendencies when I grew up, but I never witnessed the hatred and contempt before that I see between my brother and our mother.

I wonder where Makani will go in his current crazy state of mind? Is he angry and desperate enough to kill himself?

CHAPTER TWENTY-TWO

Lily

I wait by the outdoor hut covering multiple rentable surfboards at the Waiohai Beach. The resort has California-style stucco vacation glamour—pools, statues, water slides, with the ocean only steps from me. A pink and yellow plumeria tree drops fragrant blooms on my path. I pick one up and wish I could pull off the petals the way I used to pull off daisy petals and say, "He loves me. He loves me not. He loves me. He loves me not." At least then I'd have an answer at the end of the daisy. It's hard for me to trust this sweet guy. He's had zero experience with girls. I know I'm too committed to him, but I love him. I sit on the sand in the shade of a coconut palm tree to wait for him. Surfers ride the waves to my right while a father holds his baby's feet in the water. The child cries. A woman beside him wades out into the surf. She looks pregnant.

I'm a little envious. Laughing children chase the surf's playful surges. A boy jumps up and down in the tide, his eyes full of glee and his hands waving like a bird's wings. I wish to have children and a man who wants them too.

After charging my phone in the sun, I check messages. My sister wonders if I'm having a great time on the cruise ship. She asks if I've met anyone interesting. Yes. What she doesn't know will keep her from worrying. There may be a warrant out for our arrests for murder. Have I had the time of my life? Yes, in some ways. We slept in a shed and ran for our lives, but I wouldn't trade any of it. I let out a long sigh.

I check Kauai news. Kekoa comes up behind me and yells at a little redheaded girl walking toward a seal flopping up the beach to sleep on the warm, dry sand. "Get away! Get away from the seal! They bite," Kekoa says.

He runs to where the little girl stands two feet from a large seal waddling up. "Come to where I am. This seal can bite, Sweetheart."

The child looks at him as if he had said nothing. Just then, the seal snaps at her. Kekoa picks her up and brings her to the dry sand. She squirrels off from him and runs to her father.

Kekoa turns to the dad, "Seal finger is a thing because seals bite. If it goes untreated, people can lose the usage of their fingers. It's a law here to stay one-hundred-fifty feet from a seal."

"Come here, Honey," the dad says, ignoring Kekoa.

She turns her head to watch the seal as her dad drags her by the hand up to his chair.

Kekoa turns to me, but down the beach, a couple of men in swim trunks point to Kekoa and start running toward him.

It takes me a beat to realize they're gunning for him. I yell, "Kekoa, run!"

He runs up the sand to the resort's walkway and dives over a hedge. Moving like a madman, he rolls and crashes into a palm tree stump. He flips over and stands faster than my heart can beat—monkey that he is. His dark hair takes wing as he darts around a pond and more landscape plants and runs into the resort. I crouch behind a hedge and listen as the men approach and swear.

"Where'd he go?" one short, dark-haired guy asks. He wears a lemon-yellow lit-up swimsuit, as if the sunrise starts on his bum. He sees me and wiggles his eyes. Revulsion fills me, and I look away.

"Come on, in the resort," the taller one says.

The two men rush in, going through the same door Kekoa had entered.

My stomach swirls into a square knot. I sink onto the grass, pull my knees to my forehead, and pray. My paranoid side visualizes Kekoa coming out with one of Silver's minions on each side, his face bloodied because they can. I push aside the image, keep praying, and curl up to the shrub hedge.

After a few minutes, I recognize the ship's security guys coming back out the door. The taller one that I've seen on the ship leads. His square jaw is set. He walks fast. "Come on. It's time to get back to the ship, anyway. Let's not even tell Silver we saw him; otherwise, we'll catch it for losing him." The men's voices grow more distant as they walk toward the parking lot. I only catch the words, "Silver's so intense," as they walk away.

For an hour, I sit watching the entrance, but Kekoa doesn't show. I yearn for him to walk out of that door. Am I still trying to rescue men? I don't see how this can end well. But my heart longs to know him, be with him, and grow together. When he stops comparing himself to his brothers and sees that girls will flock to him, will he still choose me?

I wonder if I should just fly home and get a job until college begins next fall. The community college will have core classes I could take. Mom is lonely now that Dad's gone. I feel I have to take care of her as I always have. Why do I keep myself in this caretaking position? Boy, would it shock her to get a call about a warrant for my arrest? My cruise ship application documents my home address and emergency contacts.

Lord, redeem me. Please, don't let Silver get away with his crimes. Make a way for Kekoa to live the life You envisioned for him when You created him. You wanted him. Bless the doctor who delivered him alive. Amen.

The palm frond's fingers wave in the offshore breeze. I move to sit on the beach and enjoy the tradewinds, the soft texture of the tawny sand, and take in the teal water before me. My shoulders relax.

My brain keeps coming back to Kekoa. The way he looks after me, sleeping in the corner while I sleep on the hammock he built. He never pushes for sex. This differs from any relationship I've ever had. Scary. I can leave other guys and realize I have invested little, but with Kekoa, there are layers of his care that wrap around me and pull me close. Without him, I'm alone. Why is that?

His face projects in my mind, his amber skin, like a deep tan, the mole on his cheek. I long to study the unshaved bristles of his jaw and the high cheekbones holding his innocent eyes. Those eyes that see the best in you. The unruly eyebrows other men would have trimmed. Chapped lips I wish I could kiss. Hair that needs a cut. What guy lets his mother cut his hair?

I shuffle to the parking lot after another hour and ask for rides. A surfer lady's destination is Lihue. She drives me there, to Kukio Grove Mall, and I get off and lumber down the road, picking up the flowers that the wind blows down. An emptiness inside me cries out as cars swoosh past me. I imagine Kekoa waiting for me at the shack. I need everything to be fine. No crimes. No warrants. No restrictions. Tears fill my eyes. I want Kekoa. I want him to be free—free to love me. I want us to go to college together.

It takes a couple of hours to get to the shed. It's empty.

CHAPTER TWENTY-THREE

Kekoa

With two guys chasing me, the old pig hunt adrenaline kicks in. My dive over the shrub carried me crashing into a tree trunk, and now my head rings. I'm clueless inside this mammoth building I've never been in before. The sunroom has stations placed around the circle to sign up for different excursions. The floor's ocean wave pattern is moving, rolling, like a movie of the sea under my feet, like I'm walking on water. An elevator on my left is ready to close. I jump on it and smile at an older couple. "Hi, what's been fun?" I ask with too much enthusiasm. The little elevator has a shiny Kauai flower mural on each wall.

"Oh, well, there's a seal right out front, sleeping." The man put his hand on the handrail circling the space.

Smiling, I remember the little girl who walked up to the seal, and say, "Is that your first seal sighting?"

"Yes, it is. We've been to Maui, but this is our first time to Kauai."

On the third floor, the door opens, and they get out. I drop my smile and push the tenth-floor button. Will Silver's pawns get the hotel security to help find me? Hiding is getting old, *God. Pleeease, free me.* The flower box elevator moves from floor to floor until I land on the tenth floor. The thick carpet portrays palm fronds against a blue background. I wander past rooms alone until I notice a beehive-patterned metal floor on a sky bridge stretching to the next building. From there, I can almost touch a palm tree growing beside the span. I climb on the black handrail, hold on to a beam for balance, and jump. The limb I grab crackles but crashes me square onto the trunk. I maneuver to the back side so I'm not visible and shinny down as I've done a thousand times at home getting coconuts for Mom.

Once the two guards realize the resort's size, they're apt to give up on finding me. I circle to the front of the resort and saunter down another hotel's path to the sea. Lily's vulnerable if she's waiting for me out front. But I can't go to find her without risking being caught. I hang at the beach to the right of the resort under a canopy, blending in by sitting at the edge of a birthday party for a sixteen-year-old girl.

The adults drink beer while everyone dances in their bikinis or swim trunks. The birthday girl, Saphira, wears a gold suit that lights up. She seems to display herself like we display our fruits and vegetables on market day. I'm fascinated by how people live, but revulsion sweeps through me. Her brother bounces and moves to the music. He says to his sister, "Move your jelly body over, bxxxx." What disrespect. Saphira pretends to ignore him, dancing in front of her boyfriend. The jerk doesn't hide where he looks, but then she seems to want the attention. I'm fascinated and saddened by the dynamics.

I slip out, tie on my slippers with the strings on my trunks, and dive into the ocean. The autumn water is about 75 degrees, not warm, but once I'm in, refreshing. Yellow fish with black stripes swim close to me. If only I could clean my mind of the pictures of Saphira's curvy body gyrating to the music. After I swim around the rocks and pass Brenneke's Beach, I can relax more. Striding to shore, I ponder if I should risk showering at the public showers. By the sun's position, it must be after five. Fewer people are on the beach, and the ship should pull out now with its security personnel on it. I venture up the sandy knoll of the public beach park and shower. Mischief used to shake off after her dips in the lake. I think of her as I shake my hair. A pang of sadness floats over me. Sneaking back to where I last saw Lily, I blush with anticipation, but she's not there. After a search of the area, I give up. My hands slap my face. What have I done? She must have gotten a ride to the ship and left. A place to sit on a bench beckons me. Lily. Gone. What a difference between Saphira's body wiggling, enticing, almost offering, and the Lily I know. Know, not just see. Know. I'm not ready for her to go. Will she free herself by ending her association with me? I hope so for her sake, but my heart revolts at the thought of losing her. With jagged breathing, I say, "No. Lily, my sweet." My head leans on my bent knees. The breeze dries the sweat from my body, but my hair drips down my face.

Something brushes against my arm. I look up and see Makani.

"You okay?" he asks.

"Makani." I stand and hug him.

He hugs me. No, he clings to me.

As if it's a big favor, he asks, "Can I hang with you for the rest of the day? I told my mom I was staying with a friend tonight; you're my friend, right?" The desperation in his voice shakes me.

I smile and ruffle his hair. "Sure, I'm your friend forever." His eyes show affection but also a lostness. "Do you have your bike?"

"Yeah, back at the parking lot. If you still have Mom's, use it because she never does."

There's a walking bike path for half the way to Lihue. The evening is peaceful, with some clouds and the usual mid-seventies temperature for our fall. I love seeing the ocean from this vantage. Usually, we view beaches from our boat, not from the land. The bike path parallels the curves of the ocean, then it heads north to connect with the highway. From here, it's more hazardous because it's dusk and the bikes have poor lights. The sky has darkened by the time we reach the shed.

I open the door, and Lily screams.

"Lily, Lily, it's me, Kekoa. Makani is with me. It's okay."

I hear her feet hit the floor and her arms surround me. "Kekoa." She buries her face in my shoulder. Makani joins our hug, and the three of us cling to each other.

The smell of hamburgers and fries makes my mouth plead with me for food. I haven't eaten since this morning. "Do I smell food?"

Lily says, "I bought some food from Burgerville on the chance you'd come. Help yourselves."

Makani and I chow down. She bought drinks too. We spend the evening by the fire I build, tell stories, and sing our favorite songs. Laughter comes as easy as breathing. Makani wants to know all about our canyon. He asks, "Can you take me there? I want to live there." I wish I could take both Makani and Lily. Everyone would love them. If they're still there. My brothers might have left, then my parents, aunties, and uncles might move to where their grandkids are. Will anyone even be there now?

"What's your favorite sport?" Lily asks.

"Surfing and just swimming in the ocean," I say.

"I don't know how to swim. I'd just drown. Maybe it would be better," Makani says. His head dips.

"Well, let's fix that," I say and show him swimming techniques by the light of the campfire—how to reach out and push the water, how to flutter kick, and rotate from side to side so you can breathe without slowing your speed. In the dark, we trek down to the ocean at Small Boat Harbor, and I help him swim. He's so proud of himself. What kind of mother doesn't ensure her son knows how to swim when they live on Kauai?

When we get back, Makani and I stoke the fire, and I sit on the ground. Lily sits on a bucket she found in the shack. My new brother rolls over a rock and sits on it.

Makani says, "Why did you leave the ship?"

I explain why I had to leave, how I came to board the ship and meet Ingrid and Silver.

"It's like a crime ring. Do they have anyone on Kauai? Are you safe now that the ship's gone?" he says.

Ants are crawling on my ribs and belly, so I stand to brush them off. "Maybe Clint, the guy that set me up, came looking for someone to take the blame for their thefts. And then Ingrid gets murdered."

Makani whistles his surprise. "Clint conned you into working on the ship, pretending to be him, and blames you for Silver's thefts. Why did Ingrid have to die? What did they get out of it?"

I'm not used to thinking that way, but it makes sense. "Ingrid pretended to like me. She took me to dinner and then took my glass. Another time, she suggested we swim. She took all these videos and pictures of me and then acted as if she didn't care about me at all."

Makani looks at me. "What did she want with your glass?"

"Your DNA," Lily says.

"That's how we found you and your mom," I say.

Makani's eyes get big. "She found out who Dad is." The boy talks with his hand, explaining his theory. "Googled him and saw that he's rich. The witch scammed him, called him, and wanted money, I bet. That's why Mom has kept me a secret. Damian is married to the daughter of a billionaire. If that Ingrid girl knew about Mom and you—his son—she could blackmail him. Damian's wife would divorce him, and he'd lose it all. Dude, Mom's just his sidekick. He keeps her with promises and free rent."

"And if Silver found out, maybe he wanted in on the action, and they argued," I say.

"And he killed her," Lily says. "I can visualize him murdering for money."

Makani slouches: his chin is almost on his chest.

I ask, "Hey, Bro, you okay?"

He looks up at me. The fire reflects off a tear coming down his face. "I can't live with a mom who wants to kill her children. What does that make me, a mistake? Grandma raised me when I was a baby and then stopped. She told Mom, 'Take care of your own problem' as she used to refer to me." Makani turns around and wipes his face with his shirt. Contempt coats every word. His shoulders sink, and his head drops like his torso became wet clay. "I, I can't live this way. If I die, it's because of her." The bars of the cage she holds him in are strong with anger.

I go over and hold him. What would Mom do? She'd pray. "Lord, You planned Makani and me. You formed us with more love than the best father in all the world because You wanted us to live. Thank You that You haven't finished with us yet. Give us Your love and let that be enough for us. Amen."

Makani sobs. I hold him tight, stroking his hair the way Dad would smooth mine when he held me. "I got you, Bro. You're my brother. I'm not ever going to let you go."

Makani wipes his face with the bottom of his t-shirt again and pulls away.

I wish he didn't hate his mother. Mom's empathy techniques might help. I say, "My Mom, the counselor, used to make us guess how our brothers felt. If we didn't dig deep enough, she would make us think more about them to develop empathy. I'd like to do that with you. Pretend you're Mom, totally in love with Damian, needing his love to fill all the holes her childhood didn't and her fantasy demands. What does that feel like?"

"Don't make me do this. I want to hate her. She's a xxxxxx xxxxx!" Makani's lips purse, matching the rest of his pinched face.

"And how will hate help you heal?"

"I don't care about healing, she's a bxxxx." The boy balls his fists and hits my chest. I see mountains of pain and rejection ripping at him. Whippings that never stop.

I remember myself throwing hissy fits. My face must have looked like his. But I had two parents, no, really six parents, who loved me and spent their days and evenings giving to and developing me. "Will your hate hurt Mom and Dad?"

Makani puckers his face. He growls. "Not as much as I want it to. I'm going to call that XXXXX and tell him exactly what I think of him."

"That's not safe right now; Mom hid you for a reason," I say.

Makani turns and walks away using words I've never heard but know exactly what they mean.

CHAPTER TWENTY-FOUR

Lily

I get to sleep in the hammock as the guys sleep on the floor. All our heads are buzzing with our "Silver" theory.

The next morning, it's market day. After Makani leaves to ride his bike home, Kekoa and I hike up to Puhi, where Kekoa's family will sell their food. He's jumpy with excitement about seeing his family, even though he'll only observe from a distance. Clint may search for him at Silver's request. Kekoa should stay out of sight and watch out for the snake.

In the vast field by the highway, trucks are unpacking. People scurry to set up tables and spread their displays of yellow-orange papaya, green lettuces, cucumbers, potatoes, kale, red tomatoes, squash, and bananas of all sizes to sell. My stomach feels fuzzy thinking about meeting his family, even if we're just friends. His family's spread stands out among the others, the one run by Caucasians, not locals. One of these gray-haired women is the lady who held him, cuddled him, kissed his sprains and cuts, rocked him to sleep, prayed for him, and taught him everything he knows about women. She's the one he'll compare me to.

It's too early to buy; it's not 9:00 yet. I want them to get set up before I distract them with news of their handsome son. Two women set up tables, another talks to them and then drives off with a paper in her hand. Costco runs, of course. They only come to Lihue once a week.

I hang by the tent and listen. One wearing a teal and white muumuu says, "Almost there. It's sure not the same without Kekoa. I see local boys and think it's him. My heart wants me to chase him. But I can't. I have customers."

The second puts her hand on her friend's shoulder. "Lord, keep him safe. If you want to chase down a boy who looks like Kekoa, go right ahead. I'll cover for you." They chuckle, and she sets out a woven box full of handmade cards. My artistic juices are flowing, thinking about getting my fingers on them.

"Did Kana get the knee compression sleeves for Dad? With just two boys, it will be harder to get all the meat into the sidecars. In case Dad needs to help."

"Yeah, he did. Don't worry. They'll be fine."

The heaviness of her expression reveals she isn't fine. In a moment, I'll pull back the veil and tell them about their wonderful son.

Out of the corner of my eye, I wonder at two police cars pulling into the parking lot closest to their stand. Four officers stride toward their display. They don't walk to the women—they walk to me.

The taller of the men looks at a paper he's holding, then at me. "Excuse me, are you Lily Ann Albrecht?"

My jaw falls to my toes. I stammer, "Yes, I am." I eye them. Their faces don't seem to condemn.

"We're not arresting you, Ms. Albrecht. We just want to take you in for questioning."

"What's this about?" I glance at Kekoa's family staring at me a few feet away and regret asking. All they need is to think Kekoa is involved in some murder he didn't commit.

The female officer steps forward. "All in due time, Ma'am. Can I ensure you have no weapons?"

I nod, and she pulls out a six-inch wand and scans me. She steps back, "Alright then, let's go."

At the stucco police station, I'm escorted to an office on the second floor and settle into a metal chair with a mesh seat and back. The table is thick and plastic-looking like glass, but safer and cheaper. The room is naked of décor. I bite my chapped lips and wiggle my toes.

Officer Ishikara sits next to me with a recorder on the table. "May I record your answers?"

"Sure, I say. I'm not going to lie." *Lord, help me.*

He's buff and tan with dark smooth hair, maybe a surfer. White streaks show at his temples. "Makani Kaaumoana, a teen fifteen years old, has been reported missing. His brother, Kekoa Laskey, is under suspicion of kidnapping. What do you know about either of these boys?"

I swear under my breath. "He, Makani, told us last night his mom was fine with him spending the night with a friend. In this case, Kekoa and I were his friends. He left this morning and said he was going home."

The officer lets his breath out slowly and adjusts in his chair. "Where were you last night?"

I tell him about the shed, the brothers, their mother, and their father. He probes regarding why we left the ship, so I tell him all about Silver, Ingrid, and our theory about the security ring. His eyebrows close in. He massages his forehead and glances up at a window next to us. It must be a one-way mirror. Who is watching us?

He chews the inside of his mouth and appears to be contemplating my words. "Okay, Ms. Albrecht, you may leave. Please write your phone number down on this pad so we can ask you any more questions that come up." He pushes a pad toward me.

"Officer, Kekoa is the kindest, most innocent guy I've ever met. I know he doesn't have a chip identity of his own, but please don't send him to the military. He wants to ask his birthmother to apply for a birth certificate, social security number, and chip for him."

I write my number down.

He almost smiles. His eyes become understanding. "It's out of my power, Ma'am. But if you see him, ask him to call me. If what you're saying is true, we'll be able to clear him. He's better off working with us than facing a crime ring by himself. I'll get him in touch with the FBI. But right now, he's the prime suspect in a kidnapping. That's a felony."

"But he didn't. . .," I say.

The cop put up his hand to stop me.

"I understand. Just help us find the boy," the officer says.

I step out into the sunshine, but a storm thunders in my heart. A sense of panic fills me, realizing that I have to get to the shed before Kekoa does. The police know where it is because I told them. The police may notify Damian that his son, Makani, is missing. We need to find Makani before his birth father gets that call.

If he wants to kill Kekoa, he will want to kill Makani too. I'm a couple of miles away. Cutting through a resort, I run until my breath runs out. Will I get there in time? If Maili won't let Makani hang out with Kekoa, will he try to kill himself?

CHAPTER TWENTY-FIVE

Kekoa

At the farmer's market, I hide behind somebody's pickup cab and watch Mom talk to four law enforcement officers. Why? If only I could go talk to her. Two of the four police stay at the market and glance around. The grassy open field has only a single tree shading an entire corner, but tents fill the area with vendor's wares. I walk away, hanging close to a couple of girls so I would appear to accompany them.

"Hi." A girl with blue-colored hair pokes her friend and flashes a smile at me. She's in her twenties, I think.

"Hi, nice day for the market," I say. My voice sounds shy. I have no confidence in myself when I talk to girls I've never met.

"What's your name?" the girl beside the blue-headed one says. She's about five feet seven inches tall, thin, and wears stretch jean shorts and a tank top with flashing lights advertising a beer company.

I pause, thinking of what to say. "Laskey, what's yours?" My last name feels more distant and safer. It is not. If the detective took Lily in, they'll for sure be looking for me.

"I'm Sheryl and this is Destiny. We're from Texas on vacation. You?"

"Local."

"Really," Sheryl says. She's almost jumping up and down. "Will you be our tour guide and drive us all over the island?"

I stammer. "Ah, ah, I don't have a driver's license or a car." Lily's been arrested, and these girls want me to be a tour guide. No way.

"You don't have a driver's license? Not even for a car?" Sheryl's voice carries the hammer of shock.

My cheeks are hot. I glance about, hoping to keep them from reading my eyes.

Destiny, the older of the two, in her late twenties, with white skin wrinkling under her eyes, says, "We can rent a car, and I'll drive."

Sheryl can't let it go. "Yes!" Her forehead wrinkles. "How do you get around?"

I stare at the ground and move my tight shoulders. "My dad has a car and a boat. We use both to get around."

Sheryl stands too close to me. "Wow, will you take us out in your dad's boat?"

"No. He's hunting pigs right now, and I can't leave to give you a tour. Sorry." I am sure my face must be clown's-nose-red.

"What, hunting pigs, wild pigs?"

"Yeah, it's a thing here.

"Can you call him and see when you could use his boat?" Sheryl doesn't back off but twists her long tiger-striped hair in her fingers. I can't imagine how she got it to look that way. Her eyes plead with me—they have claws.

How can I say it? I blurt out, "I don't have a phone."

Sheryl shakes her head. "Not everyone has wireless earphones, but everyone has a phone. You don't? Not even a hand-held? Are you homeless and on drugs?" Her voice carries an air of contempt, or perhaps disbelief. Or she thinks I am lying.

Destiny laughs. "Yeah, right? Who doesn't have a phone?"

I walk away stung as if I'd swallowed a hive of aloneness.

It takes all my willpower to walk in the opposite direction from where my mom is selling food. Each foot moves ahead, wanting to rebel and find Mom. My mother treasured all my stick figure drawings. She bought me cowboy boots when I wanted them after seeing Toy Story on an ancient DVD. Her smile reassured me every time I entered the room. I don't want to be different. I want to be a normal person with a chip and go home.

My feet turn toward the beach—where I go when my insides need a place to break loose. With Lily gone, I wonder if I should hide in the jungle and try to make a hut somewhere. If I caused Lily to be arrested, I'll hate myself. My fists clench and shake up and down.

By the time Nawiliwili Bay comes into view, sweat drips down my forehead. My tongue sticks to the roof of my mouth. Maybe the trash has a half-drunk water bottle. Instead of going up toward the fishpond, I stroll along the beach in front of Duke's oceanfront restaurant and tell God about my dilemma. At the other end of the boardwalk, a drinking fountain quenches my thirst.

I pick my way past the port and into the trees and brush and walk toward the shed, worried about being followed. Branches crunch, but when I peer, nobody's there. I've passed all the houses and condos. No one could hear me yell here in the Guinea grass and shrubs.

There's a hill to my right and a steep decline to my left. If I jump down, someone higher could spot me. I tuck behind a haole koa shrub with its feathery branches. Bean pods hang down, brown and dry, reminding me of dead needles on a Christmas tree. I wait. Faint walking noises come my way. There's a vague beeping sound unfamiliar to me. The sound gets closer. A man talks to someone, but I can't make out what he's saying. The steps come closer. Two or three voices mumble to each other. I hold my breath. My calf cramps, and I sit and massage them. Did I make too much noise?

My heart trampolines. It bounces so high I can almost feel it breaking the surface of my skin.

Their steps are on the dirt road in front of me now. They stop.

A click. "Send the bird." The voice is in front of me. Why a bird?

I can't see him. Holding my breath, I hope he doesn't notice me. Why did he stop right in front of me? I don't wear anything someone could track. A PlanePod whines closer. It stops dead in front of me. The thing lowers to the ground. The vibrations of the wind coming from it blow the shrub like a windstorm and send a chill down my spine.

"Go," a man says. The branch in front of me moves, revealing me. I jump back to run, but some beast tackles me to the ground. He's heavier than either of my brothers. I lie face down in the grass as a big Samoan man pulls my hands behind my back and ties them with a rope. I turn and spot another just as big next to him. The man who tackled me hauls me to my feet. I turn around. The second man holds a heat sensor scanner. They found me with it. I'm ready to spring up and run, but with no arms. *God, what is this with having my hands bound?*

"Keep quiet and climb in the PlanePod, or I'll make you wish you were never born," the jerk says.

Time stands still, but my breathing is fast and shallow. A push toward the door by one of the brutes bumps me forward. My movements are rigid, like I can't move. The flying car can't carry the two giants and me. They're figuring that out when I jerk away from my kidnapper and dive headlong down the hill toward the fishpond.

If I curl and roll, the momentum will keep going. I slam into the ground, hitting the back of my neck and my shoulders. The momentum straightens me out and my hips bang against the dirt. I can't protect my skull, but I roll sideways and curl again, pushing off with my neck muscles, then trying to tuck my chin to my chest. My body slams, bangs, and bounces down the hill. Over and over, my hands slam against the ground, tied behind me as my body rolls. I curl my fingers into a fist to keep from breaking a bone. Rocks and sticks skewer my skin. I hear swearing above me, but I try again and again to roll to a stand, so I control where I go. There is no control flying down the hill. I bang on a bigger rock, cutting my scalp, but on I roll. This is worse than being underwater and being spun by a wave because my body keeps slamming into the earth and rocks. I lie sideways at the bottom, dizzy and disoriented. The mini helicopter hums by me, looking for a place to land.

There's no time to think. I manage to stand, run to the pond, and dive in. I can dolphin kick at least. But there's no missing me. I am the biggest fish in the pond—the one who has to breathe air. The water is dirty from recent rains bringing silt downstream. It tastes of rotten fish and soil. I kick to the other side of the pond. It's so slippery, I step on the side to stand and slide back in again. *Please God, get me out of here.* Again and again, I try to scamper up the bank but slip. On the ground, I roll, lying prone. It's so hard to roll uphill, but it works. The mud covers me. Voices come closer as men encircle the pond to capture me. To drag me to their PlanePod. What then? Death? These are not police. The thugs must work for Damian or Silver.

I roll into the river next to the pond. They could follow me, but they can't land on the rough south-side terrain of the river. I kick into the current. A gunshot hits the water next to me, and I dive. *Lord, they're trying to kill me. Help.*

By staying in the fast-moving center of the river, I zip downstream. My lungs scream. The PlanePod whizzes overhead back and forth, no doubt with men hanging out the windows with guns. They'll need to shoot me soon because there are people on the beaches in the bay ahead of me. There are laws prohibiting flying off designated areas. Unless it's a racing area, they have to fly over the roads because of privacy.

I swim toward the outer edge of the stream, which pushes me into a circular eddy. When the circle rounds toward the shore, I roll up onto the gravel and creep several feet behind a rock formation, gasping for breath. The bolder is about eighteen inches tall, with small rocks behind it that had rolled down the cliff above me. I try to kick the loose rocks away to make room to hide. The rocks cut my legs and bare feet, but I keep kicking. The human drone machine hums toward me. Like a crazy man, I curl behind the boulder, shaking. I don't want to die. Awful choking sounds come from my throat. My face presses against the dirt and rocks. I breathe in dust and cough. Lord, this is wrong. This is so very wrong. Why do people want to kill me? Why?

CHAPTER TWENTY-SIX

Lily

When I arrive at the shack, no one is there. Kekoa and Makani might be at the Farmer's market, so I race there. The vendors are packing up. I search for Kekoa, but he's disappeared. Who knows what he thinks happened? My shoulder blades pinch, so I try stretching to relieve the pain. Kekoa's family pulls totes out of their van and fills in the empty spots on the tables with more food. My blood pressure must zoom looking at them, knowing this is my chance. I suck in a deep breath and march over.

Two boys about Kekoa's age take down tables while a gray-haired man unties the tent canopy. "Hi. Do you have a minute? I'm a friend of Kekoa's. He loves you all so much. I think you're the most loving family in the world."

Every person in his family stops what they're doing and stares at me. Disbelief. Shock. Hope. Sorrow. A million emotions fly through their eyes in a nano-second.

His mother unfolds two chairs leaning against a pole and sets them up. She offers me one of them. "Please tell me your name." Tears stream down the wrinkled creases on her face. She closes her eyes as if she's trying not to cry, but the tears flow. Her husband comes up behind her.

"What's that? Did you say 'Kekoa'?" His voice is gentle, but with ripples of disbelief inside.

"Yes, well, I should start from the beginning, so it all makes sense." I rub my fingers along the fabric of my shirt like I do when I'm stressed.

Both guys come and sit at my feet. One looks like a surfer, blond, tan, and buff. He must be Canyon. The other, Kana, is lanky, with shiny black hair. He seems to take in every detail but is more aloof than Canyon, who looks as if he wants to sit on my lap with his smile.

I tell them everything I know, and they listen. Kekoa's mother keeps asking me to slow down because when I talk, my mouth goes into high gear. Everyone else leaves the field, but we're still there an hour later. Kekoa's mom cries through it all. His dad rubs her back as he stands behind her. He's teary too. The boys lean in, not letting one word go unheeded.

Kana asks how-things-work questions all the way through, but Canyon says, "Whoa" to everything I say.

Dad hesitates. He starts to speak and then stops. He says, "Would you like to pray for Kekoa with us, Lily?"

"Sure," I say. We form a circle and hold hands.

"Lord, our Redeemer," Kekoa's mom starts, her voice shaking, "protect and guide our son. Let him own Your victory, even before he sees it. You who have overcome the world bring Kekoa the faith and actions to overcome those who plot against him. Bring him safely back to us."

Each person prays. I notice each one dropping hands periodically to wipe away tears. I have goosebumps; "chicken skin," Kekoa calls it. The boys' hands are smooth and strong. Their long fingers with dirty fingernails clench a family member's hand. Streaks of pig blood still mark Canyon's arms.

Kekoa's mom's gnarled hands with purple veins that bubble up have skin so thin and spotted it doesn't hide the color of the veins. Bumps stand out on her swollen knuckles, and her nails are short and unpolished. Her body is spent, worn out, given to these, her treasures, her sons. I pray he comes back to her, to them. To me. Tears dampen my cheeks. What if Silver, Damien, or the military catches him?

CHAPTER TWENTY-SEVEN

Kekoa

A s if fishhooks snag in my brain, jerking from every direction, my head throbs. Because of my somersaults down the long hill and the rocks and sticks that cut me, pain ripples up and down my spine. I massage my temple, but it doesn't help. My stomach rolls and lurches. I vomit through my mouth and nose. The flying car whizzes by again. All I can do is cower close to the rock and try to stay still. *Please, Lord, don't let them spot me.*

Once the craft flies upstream, I stagger out and dive into the current. Muddy river water tastes better than what's in my mouth right now. I hold my breath and swim underwater into the current. The cool stream seems to help my headache a bit, but in the saltwater-river water mix, my back and leg cuts are tiny searing stabs. I swim into the riptide and let it take me. The thugs fly overhead and dive closer to the water. With my lungs burning, I have to breathe. My arms rip at the water until I break the surface. A gasp later, I dive underwater again.

The PlanePod's buzz gets louder. The muddy water makes visibility difficult. I pray they can't spot me. The ocean water changes. Cleaner salt water from the ocean, warmer than the mountain stream, infiltrates the river. My cuts sting like I've rolled in a beehive with added salt. Small Boat Harbor must be on my left. I swim underwater to the side and follow the bay. When I come up for air, I notice the buzz of the aircraft flying over the river's beaches where I have just been. The PlanePod passes over me and stops. They see me! Another PlanePod, teal, with ocean waves painted over it, flies over the parking area. The killers above me fly off, knowing they're not allowed to fly over the streams. The teal PlanePod saved my life. It hums away, oblivious. *Thank You, God, for bringing help!*

A grassy area edges a rocky knoll above me. There are bathrooms as well. Many homeless individuals live out of their cars and choose to stay here. The restrooms won't be clean. My head jackhammers still, and my intestines punch me. It's hard to think. I lie on the small-rocked beach, flop from side to side like a fish out of water and catch my breath. It's too visible from overhead to stay long. But while the thugs are not near me, I need to breathe. They may come back since the teal PlanePod has gone. I try to stand, but I fall backward into the wet rocks.

The drumming of my heart—a rock band on drugs—alarms me. As I slip on the silt trying to stand again, I bend my knees to anchor my footing. I'm woozy, and the ground rollercoasters, like I'm flying down the zipline. Something circles me and then presses against my face. Something is weird. My head spins.

Yipping sounds awaken me more. Suntan lotion scent brings me memories of surfing on the North Shore. Then I notice yellow painted toenails on pretty feet sinking into the muddy sand next to me.

A young woman pulls a leaf off my face. "Dang, you look terrible. Do you want me to call an ambulance?" Her feet disappear, but the dog keeps barking at me.

Words have to spin around my brain for a while before I can say them. "No, thank you." I roll onto my back. What if I lost my swim trunks in the river? My hand goes to my hips to touch my shorts. I relax, feeling them in place, and stare up at her. Her brown hair seems crowned by a golden halo of the sun shining through the top of her head.

"Hi."

I am too weak to waste energy on feeling stupid.

"How did you manage to look as if you've been over a few waterfalls before beaching like a seal? And what's with your hands tied behind your back?"

"You got a month for me to tell you the story?" I sit up and glance around. Puffy white cumulus clouds shoot around the sky. My chin drapes over my knees as I summon the energy to stand and reassure this girl.

She helps me walk to a picnic table and offers me a bottle of water. "I didn't get your name. My name is Gardenia. Poly and I come here for walks every day after I get off work. I haven't seen you here before. You live around here?"

Whatever I say will encourage more questions. "I'm only staying for a week. Man, that current is strong. To swim here with my hands tied on a dare almost got the best of me."

"Kalapaki Beach is only a mile away," she says.

Yeah, I know. "That's a better idea. Thanks." Poly's tail beats faster than the guitar strum of a rock song. Drinking water helps. I notice interest in me when I glance up at the girl's green eyes and sunburned face. She looks like she's in her mid-twenties. "Boy, who would have thought a seventeen-year-old could be so stupid?"

Gardenia straightens and gives me a sad smile. "Yeah, well, don't do it again. See ya." She puts Poly on the ground and waves goodbye.

I don't know how long it's been since I collapsed on the beach. Damian might hire a crew to comb the beaches and search for me. My backside reminds me of when my brothers and I created a mudslide pouring into our stream. But my open sores reveal—I'm not home. Where can I hide? My heart collects steel weights when I think about the danger I've put Lily in, the thugs trying to kidnap me, Makani's emotional crisis, and the imminent danger of Damian wanting to kill my brother and me. How can I get this to stop? Blood drips down my back, attracting flies. The rocks ripped my trunks in the back. My abrasions and cuts are small, except for a deep cut on my right shoulder. Who would stop all this? Damian is in California but could hire criminals. If I talk to the police, they'd hold me for the military. Would Maili ever turn Damian in?

I head across the grass park to Maili's house. If she sees me all cut up and hears how Damian is trying to kill me, she might change her mind. She tried to protect me once. I have to get a birth certificate and become human. My head jackhammers its booming, pulsing pain. Maybe she'll know where Lily is.

If Lily went back on the ship, I'll never see her again. I lean against a tree and sink to the trunk. Lily. My whole body shakes, even my brain is muddy. I collapse to the ground. Lily. Please find me. Please don't leave me.

Chloroform smell against my face. *Lord, help...*

CHAPTER TWENTY-EIGHT

Lily

I stroll downhill as if I don't have a care in the world. As if the man I love isn't being hunted down. A giant carrot peeler has cut my heart into strips. I can't walk away from my relationship with Kekoa. It's so unfair. *God, protect him and indict Silver and his creeps.* The world as I've known it has gone to Hades. I walk up from where the ship pulled away just hours ago—my life as a childcare expert with it. There will be other jobs. There will never be another Kekoa.

People walk by me eating, and my stomach demands food too. Kettle O'Fish's wafted tentacles of fresh French fries and batter-fried fish lures me in. It's in a three-story mall with an ocean view of the bay. A glass of cold water dripping down the sides is a luxury compared to living off the land. I savor every bite smothered in fish sauce. The cook used fresh ahi, the Hawaiian word for tuna, tender and flavorful.

The sea sprinkles its glittering lights across the bay. Wispy and billowy clouds crowd along the horizon. *God, what do I do now? I miss my family, and I miss Kekoa. My stomach spirals when I think of him and Makani.*

I listen for God's inner voice. Peace settles me, though my world is in chaos. "Get yourself another cellphone," I sense God saying. That feels right. I would be able to call my mom. I am sure she's worried because of me not picking up her calls.

As I make the trek to the phone store, the same car keeps passing me. I'm afraid he's going around and coming back. Am I being followed? I do what Kekoa would do; I climb behind a hedge and pull away leaves to peek through. My knees get dirty, but that's better than being abducted. Minutes drag. Then I see the white Jeep slowing down, and I see the huge driver. He must be seven feet tall. His car creeps up the hill, making other cars wait. My heartbeat kicks my chest as if it's a toddler throwing a tantrum.

The Jeep returns from the other direction and turns on a side street. After a while, he comes out on the other end of the neighborhood. Now I know why God wants me to pick up a new phone. I am helpless without it.

While the Jeep finds somewhere to turn and circle back, I knock on the door of the house I hide beside, but no one answers. I jog to the nearest street, going perpendicular to the road the Jeep has been patrolling. A gray Honda pulls out with a teen boy at the wheel. I stand in front of him.

He rolls down his window.

"I'm so sorry to bother you," I say. "There's a creep in a white Jeep following me. Wherever you're going, do you mind if I tag along?"

"Hop in," he says and looks down the road.

We go to Costco. The phone store is a short distance away. *Thank You, God.*

Once I have the phone set up, I walk out and there's the white Jeep down in the parking area. The thug isn't looking, so I circle the building and cross the highway. The mad woman that I am. How could he find me? Can you set trackers for someone's social security number through her chip?

My imagination dives into this scenario where the thugs are after Kekoa. Since I've been hanging out with him, they're after me to catch him. A car coming around a corner doesn't see me and honks at me for making him brake as I run across the road. The Kilohana lodge and restaurant are on my left, and I need to stay around people to be safe. I jog through the vast green landscaped grounds. The giant man must have seen that I've moved by now.

My sides are killing me, but I sprint on. The lodge-like restaurant is too exposed, with tables in the courtyard. A train behind the restaurant takes passengers on tours, so I buy a ticket and board. The cars are half full of tourists. Locals wear shorts, a t-shirt, or muted aloha shirt, and flip-flops they call slippers. Tourists wear new-looking bright clothing and hats. A couple from Tennessee sits by me, their drinks in hand.

The train whistles, and off we go. The person in the Jeep didn't wear a police uniform, so he's either a Damian thug or a hired Silver criminal. I stop shaking enough to call the police officer who interviewed me and explain my situation.

His voice tells me he doesn't believe my story. He tells me to come to the station and assumes I have a car.

The couple sitting next to me are from Tennessee and on their honeymoon. I look at wedding pictures on their phones and listen to the spiel the tour guide gives. We pet the donkey, try not to step in its poo, and see the sugarcane and a myriad of tropical fruit trees. If my stomach would calm down, I might enjoy the tour. But being hunted by a killer doesn't bring me peace.

The couple is staying at a resort in Kapa'a on the east coast of the island. I ask them if I can hitch a ride in their car, and they agree.

In the parking lot after the tour, I don't look around. Alex and Jenna, the couple, might suspect something's up. They're going out to dinner, so they drop me off.

I dial Mom, but I don't have enough cell reception in this area of Kapa'a. If a phone can't track, the criminals chasing me can't track me either. That's why God wanted me to buy a phone, so I could find a safe place.

Several palm trees sway in the breeze on the beach in front of a restaurant. I stop and listen to a skilled guitarist play and sing Hawaiian pop music. Kekoa sings like that. It stirs my longing for him even more.

My alcoholic dad gave me a template for a man that's all wrong. Kekoa has self-control and puts others he cares about ahead of himself. His words ring true. I should forgive my father. While I hold Dad "guilty," I get to punish him. It gives me false power and control. I hoped my judgment of him would make the hurt less, but the opposite happens. It only keeps the wound open and bleeding. I throw a stick into the tide and watch it go out to sea. There. Go—judgment. I have a new template now.

As the sun pulls back its light, it closes a curtain to my old bitterness. The silhouettes of the palm trees against the sky mesmerize me. I walk up the bike path, parallel to the tide, until I get to the north end of Kapa'a at a hostel where I check in.

My wrist swipes my information into their scanner. Another machine that knows where I am. This wasn't such a good idea. Adelle, the receptionist, is friendly but lists off the rules in her sergeant's voice.

"Hi. You're pretty," says a stocky person with short black hair sitting on a couch next to me. I'm not sure if the person is a man or a woman.

"Thank you," I say. The room holds a long table for dining. There are beater couches along the edges of the room facing the front of the media wall. A couple of middle-aged women are arm-in-arm on a couch watching a romance movie with earphones. A hiker dude, wearing boots, white socks, shorts, and a gray t-shirt, sits on a bench and pours over a map on the dining room table. The walls have outdated Kauai movie posters cheaply framed without a sense of balance in the room.

"You can sit by me." My new friend pats the couch next to him or her. The person has eye liner around their eyes.

I need friends right now. "Hi, I'm Lily. What brings you to Kauai?"

His mouth only partially turns up. "My name is Trey. My partner died last month. Staying in Tulsa held too many memories."

"I'm sorry. Tell me about them." I pause and pat his arm.

"Buddy was my golden retriever dog. He slept with me, ate with me, and cuddled with me when I watched movies. And he got older and older. Bud choked on a piece of chicken I gave him."

"Oh no. What did you do?"

"I didn't know what to do. Straddling him and pulling up his chest like you would a human to do a Heimlich maneuver didn't work. Even though I tried to dig it out with my finger, nothing I tried worked. He died in my arms." Trey looked down at his splayed fingers, tears rolling down his white cheeks. "I couldn't stop it. He died. Bud was the only one who accepted me just as I am."

I put my hand on his shoulder. A balmy silence stretches over the two of us.

He put his hand on top of mine. "Your turn. Why did you come to Kauai?"

How could I not be open with him when he'd just shown me the deepest part of his heart? "I don't know if you'll believe it. It's hardly believable. I left home to work on a cruise ship and save money for college."

"That sounds like fun."

I grunt. "You work all the time. Sleep, eat, work, repeat. It's your job to make it fun for the passengers, but not for yourself. But that's okay, I was making money. Then I met Kekoa."

"Oh, I can tell already you like him."

I smile. "Yes, I like him a lot, but he doesn't have an identity chip."

"How is that possible? I thought everyone got a chip when they were born."

"He," I pause and follow a big man lumbering across the room carrying a backpack, his toes pointing out as he walks. I'm telling Kekoa's secrets. "He was a failed abortion."

"No, how did you meet him then? Without an ID, he couldn't buy a ticket. He couldn't get paid."

"Right. A guy gave it to him, only it was a trap. These guys, security for the ship, are running a ring, stealing from passengers, and blaming it on Kekoa."

"Poor guy." His empathy sounds genuine.

"So, we jumped ship and swam to Kauai."

"It sounds like a movie to me." He chuckles and rubs his hands together.

"Now they're blaming the murder on Kekoa, and I may be an accomplice. I don't know where Kekoa went, and an immense man in a white Jeep followed me earlier today."

"Oh, you're scaring me now." His hand rose to his mouth, and his eyes swept the room.

"I'm scaring me too," I say.

Trey stands. "Let me see if we're full and if any enormous men have joined us."

"Great." I rub my legs. A friend. *Thank You, Lord.*

He returns. "We're full. No giant types have checked in. You're safe. At least for tonight. But what about tomorrow?"

"I don't know."

CHAPTER TWENTY-NINE

Kekoa

L ike in a dream, someone lifts my rubber arms and
drags me across the ground, hurting my heels. I need
to wake up; this is real. A door shuts. I'm lying,
pushed against a barrier on both sides. My head is curled by
something hard behind it. I open my eyes, and a whirr seems
to vibrate through my body. My grogginess drops off like a
dip into ice water. I stare at the leather backseat of a PlanePod
and realize the Samoan guy is in the seat by my feet. I dip my
head again and pretend to be out. We're in the air; I can't
jump out or hope to fight this guy. Teriyaki chicken scents
hit me from someone's leftover takeout somewhere in the
PlanePod. I should be hungry, but my gut is in my throat. I
must form a plan. *God, give me a plan.*

In a few minutes, the PlanePod lands. I peek and catch
a glimpse of the blue sky. As the doors arc up to open, the

giant grips my arm. I inhale the salt air and relax to pretend I'm still out. The driver walks away, but another man's foot taps me. I don't respond. The driver opens something, shuts it, and returns. They stuff me inside a canvas bag.

"For hands," the beast says.

"No need," a base voiced man says. "He's tied."

"If he moves, step on his throat. Snap da neck."

"Why don't we shoot him now instead of throwing him into the water?"

"Drowning in da ocean makes look like it's his bad. If the police discover a bullet in his head, ow-wee, they come lookin.' But if he moves—break da neck. No, take chance. Silver no care how he dies; just get picture."

The beasts dump me on the ground and turn me face up. Waves crash close. We may be at Ahukini Pier's parking lot by the lack of trees in my glimpse. An airplane flies over, confirming my guess. I have chicken skin from fear. *No, God. Mom and Dad didn't spend these years pouring into me for me to die now. I want to make a difference in the world and become the man You can make me into.*

They tie the bag and carry me. I am sure they're going to throw me into the sea. The sounds of waves crashing are loud. Each man has an end. My coffin sags in the middle. If I struggle, they'll break my neck. They don't walk out very far on the pier before the deep-voiced man says, "Pau, far enough. Let's throw da bugga as far as we can."

My arms pull on the rope binding my hands with all my strength, but it holds. I twist my hands and yank but can't free myself. The sack swings back and forth and then they launch me into the sea. I gasp as the water soaks through the sack. They must believe I've drowned to stop hunting me. The canvas fills up. Every ounce of me is on fire with adrenalin. I pull again and again in every direction to free my hands. I float because my lungs are full of air. That has to change before I can pretend to drown. *Okay, God, here's to trusting You.*

I exhale and let myself sink, and then dolphin kick to the rocks underwater. I can't see, so when I crash against the bottom, I struggle to locate a sharp-pointed rock with my feet. My lungs long for air, but I know I can hold my breath for over three minutes. My brothers and I had contests growing up. With my feet, I find a sharp rock, but as I kick the bag on both sides of the rock, the current moves me. I try again, curling over a rock just above a lower rock my feet are using as a wedge to create an opening. As my feet kick down, waves push me. But my kick rips it a bit. I have to breathe; my lungs are screaming. Once more, I kick. *Please, God.* It rips. I put a foot through, but without hands to work myself out, all I can do is kick. Both feet slide through. By squatting, I grasp the side of the canvas with my fingertips and then jam my feet out. Half of me is through. My lungs are on fire. Panic fills me. Squatting again, I feel for the opening with my fingers. I must breathe. The waves turn me over and over. "Keep your head, Son," I hear Dad saying in my head. I curl and grasp the tied end of the bag with my feet to pull myself through the hole. I am free. My feet kick before I even tell them to. The light shows above with the waves reflecting it at different angles. By following the rocks, I emerge close to shore. I hope the two men aren't looking. All the stones in the water are worn smooth by the surf, but if I climb up the rock pile to find a sharp edge to cut my hands loose, I'll expose myself. I slip and fall against my ribs on the rocks. *Please God, help me unloose my hands.*

The rocks are slick. If I can find clean sharp rocks, I can work my hands free of these ropes. It's hard to find rocks where the breakwater hasn't smoothed the boulders. Although I am exposing myself, at least there's a boulder between the men and me. Saltwater has softened the rope, so I shave away at it. A rush of excitement zips through me. The rope comes off.

I peek and see the men holding the rope attached to the bag they think still encases me. They're going to pull my dead carcass in. Surprise! The smaller guy has his cell phone in his hand. I slip into the water and pull the bag into the tide farther and put a few stones in it. If I swim to the surface to breathe, they will target me, but my lungs scream at me for air. I drop it and swim underwater to the shore again. I gasp for breath quietly, but they don't seem to hear me over the waves and breeze. *Thank You, Lord.* I rest my head against the rock and relax. A river of stress pours off me. The rise and fall of the waves may expose me, so I swim south, out of sight. I won't die today. *You want me to live out the life You have for me—I am Yours. Thank You, God.* A warmth and excitement fill me. I bested these guys with the help of the Lord and a sharp rock.

After a few minutes, a distance away, they pull the sack back, ready to take a picture of my dead body—it's full of rocks. They swear at each other for not bounding my hands and feet, or for not just killing me before they threw me in. The small man calls. I see him hold the phone away from his head and hear someone yelling at him. The smaller man's hand balls into a fist, and he punches the big guy. The big guy picks him up by his armpits and throws him backward. He falls on the rock pile and swears his sewer words as if those are the words he uses most often. The phone flies out of his fist and into the boulders. It's hard not to laugh. I slip down into the water and swim away from their cursing.

When I come up for air, the PlanePod starts and flies over the beach in front of me, illegally driving away from the road. Of course, they don't care about the law. I turn and swim underwater toward the lighthouse. When I need to breathe, I let my legs drop and only surface with my nose and mouth, then continue. The coast guard will nail them if they try to fly over the bay. I am exhausted when I realize I'm safe. For the moment, anyway. Exhausted, I become an underwater buoy, bobbing up and down, resting. A thousand baby waves rise and fall in my new world, surrounding me, supporting me, surrendering to my kicks and strokes. The ocean is the handiwork of God's hand. Flow with Him, and He enables you to see worlds you didn't know were possible. Deny Him, and you are clueless about the magic behind everything that touches you.

I reach a buoy and stop to evaluate. The tide is going in, pushing me into the bay. The sky darkens. My stomach rumbles, and I can't wait to find some food. Swimming toward shore, when I get out of breath, I tread water to watch for the PlanePod. Fortunately, they're noisy. Confident I have a few more hours to live, I continue and drag myself out in front of the resort at Kalapaki Bay. The free-standing shower next to the boardwalk feels great, even if the water is lukewarm. Hundreds of swimsuit-clad tourists walk the boardwalk, swim in the resort's sculptured pool, and lounge on the sand or in the ocean. I dig into my secret pocket on the inside of my shorts, almost tasting a steak dinner, but my cash has worked its way out of the pocket and into the ocean. All I have. Gone. I stare at the sea as if it might give it back.

Tourists on the beach ignore me, a half-drowned rat slithering up from the ocean, but I see a couple of police coming down the boardwalk looking at people as if they have a search warrant. I long to jump into a hot tub, but I walk just behind a guy going to the parking lot in the opposite direction from the police. Once in the parking lot, I jump behind a shrub and hide. It's not long before I drift off to sleep.

I awaken in the night, cold. Mosquitoes are feasting on my bare chest and legs. Sometimes hotel guests leave their hotel-striped towels out. Around the circular pool with statues, fountains, and an island in the middle, in a corner under a table, I find a wadded-up towel, missed by the cleaning crew. I take it to my bed of ground coverings and lay on it.

Right now, Lily might be helping drunks get back to their cabins. Or would Silver pull her in and arrest her? How would she find out if he suspects her of stealing Ingrid's badge and/ or helping me? I try to relive walking with her on the deck, asking her questions and studying those intriguing eyes.

I have to eat. If another restaurant would let me work for a share of the tips, I could at least live and try to get my birth mother to change her mind about me. Tomorrow, I'll try Duke's, the restaurant at the other end of the boardwalk.

Makani filters into my mind. I smile. My baby brother. Will the thugs search for him now since I've squirmed out of their reach?

If the Samoans found and killed Makani and took a picture to show it was me, neither Damian nor Silver would know the difference. I have to find Makani and protect him.

CHAPTER THIRTY

Lily

I order a lime aid and sit on the deck of the Kai and Chai pastry shop with a fresh malasada, a Portuguese version of the donut without a hole. With my new phone, I call Mom. She doesn't pick up. I leave a message, relieved she's not there to give me flack. "Hi, Mom, it's me, and this is my new phone number. I quit my job on the ship and am hanging out on Kauai. I'm okay, but please pray for my friends, Kekoa and Makani. They need it right now. Love you, bye."

I won't tell her about the weird stuff. Otherwise, she'd want me to stop all this nonsense and come home. With trepidation about what I will find, I walk toward Maili's house wearing the new jean shorts and a teal shirt I picked up at the mall.

Mom will want me to move home but going back reminds me of being fourteen again. I don't want to be fourteen. Kekoa is only seventeen, almost eighteen, but he seems so much more mature. He's spent his years learning instead of being entertained—novel thought.

A plumeria tree pokes its leafless limbs over a homeowner's cement brick fence. One bloom hangs down low enough, and I leave the road's edge to smell it. The six petals swirl in yellow, pink, and white with no stamens drop into my fingers from the tree branch. It smells light and sweet, with a unique splash of heaven.

I'd give anything to have a mom and dad who love each other as much as Kekoa's parents. Kekoa acts clueless to the social norms of today, can't read girls well, but knows how to do all this stuff nobody around me knows how to do. And he cares, not just pretends. His love for God and people uproots me with surprise. Everyone else around sucks at loving, listening, and supporting. I want to be loved with that kind of love and learn how to love like Kekoa.

With the flower tucked behind my ear, I find local news and weather on my phone. Mid to high seventies, with partly cloudy skies, scattered showers are likely from Kapa'a north. Yeah, that's every day here.

There's an amber alert; someone has kidnapped a boy. I zoom in on his picture. Makani. I stop walking. Other than his picture and where to contact if he's sighted, the article says little else. Have Damian's minions captured him, or did he run away? I call the police station, but they won't give me any information. I jog toward the highway. If my mother thought I hitched rides, she would freak out. I'm not thrilled about it either—but rideshare is expensive and not always available. Tourists often hit Costco before going to their condos or resorts, so I go there.

During the next hour, I greet shoppers in the parking lot and ask them how they like Hawaii and where they're staying. If all goes well, I ask if I can hitch a ride to Poipu. My sweat level climbs with my fear that Makani may already be dead as time creeps forward.

Magenta and Skylar are on their baby moon, playing before the baby comes. I help them pack their goods into the car and tuck myself in their rental rear seat, happy to get a ride. They're from Maine. This is their first time on Kauai. I fill them in on the local lingo—pupus are appetizers. Slippers are flip-flops. Makai means toward the sea. Mauka refers to the mountainside of the road. I learn about the baby, but the time drags. The clock stays at 4:03 for an hour before it moves to 4:04.

I tell them about the trees we pass because Kekoa told me. The albizia with the white trunk and the broad, flat canopy came from Africa and Indonesia but is invasive here.

Some fool brought it to burn to make electricity without finding out that it has shallow roots and falls over, landing in the rivers and ocean.

They drop me off on Poipu road, and I sprint to Maili's house.

I knock, and my hands go to my knees while I catch my breath.

"Lily, where is he?" Maili screams. She steps outside. "Where is Makani? You know."

I stand, unable to speak. Her eyes, swollen and pink, show she's been crying. Her hair is frizzy. I see a thin strip of gray on her scalp while the rest is black. Her shirt is one of those cooling tanks, but she still smells sweaty.

"Kekoa took him." Maili rants worse than a severe storm. "He took advantage of Makani and kidnapped him. I'm sure of it. The cops even have a warrant out for him."

"Wait. Is the warrant out for Makani or Kekoa?" I ask.

She explodes in an exasperated "Ahhhh!" She shakes her head. "Kekoa took Makani. He did." The woman is inches from my face with breath that smells of rum.

"Why do you say that?"

"Because… because Makani admired Kekoa so much. He wanted to be with him. Makani's always wanted siblings."

Maili sunk backward and leaned against her peach-colored porch. A red-flowered hibiscus plant blooms in the corner by her feet.

I put my hand on her arm. Kekoa would give her empathy right now. She's terrified. "You must be so afraid."

She drops her chin to her chest. "I'm sorry. It's not your fault. Come in." Maili opens the door, and we sit on opposite sides of their cream couch. She turns up the air conditioner.

I say, "We spent some time together. Makani wanted to stay with Kekoa. But we sent him home. He told you he was spending the night with a friend."

"I remember."

"Well, we were friends. But we told him to go home the next day. If he never came home, then he decided not to or something happened to him. It wasn't Kekoa's fault."

She gained steam again—a broken record. "Kekoa took advantage of him. He came out of the blue, won my son over, and took him away from me."

I wiggle my feet, not wanting to show my frustration. "Was Makani frustrated before Kekoa showed up?"

"Yes, but that boy put fire in him."

I can't keep my feet still. "That boy—you mean Kekoa?"

"Yes, it's hard for me. For years after the abortion, I dreamed I heard a baby crying. Just a faint cry and then gone. Like he was real and alive, then dead. Every night, I wanted him. I wanted Damian and me to be together with our baby. I waited and pleaded with Dame." Maili pulls her knees into her chest and hugs them. Tears sweep her cheeks. "I wanted him, but Damian wouldn't have it. He sent a woman who took me to the clinic." Maili breathes a jagged breath and stares out the window. "She said either I clean out my uterus, or Damian would take the house and my allowance away and never see me again." Her forehead butts over and over against her knees. "What could I do?" she asks, as if trying to convince herself. "What could I do?" She wipes her eyes. "The next time I got pregnant, I didn't tell Damian and had the baby. I couldn't go through that again."

My hand rests on her shoulder. She's been through so much guilt and shame, regret, and rejection.

After a few minutes, she sits and stares out the window again.

"Do you think Damian loves his son, Makani?" *Please God, open her eyes.*

She stiffens and swears. "No, he doesn't know about him!" She screams. "Don't you tell him, or he'll kill Makani, or me."

I hate trying to talk to hysterical people, especially when they're in denial. "Who is more apt to hurt Makani? Kekoa, his brother who loves him, or Damian? Makani said he was going to call his dad and chew him out. If Damian is trying to kill Kekoa, he will have to kill Makani too, or someone could leak the news to his wife."

Her eyes bolt open as she glares at me. "No, Damian would never hurt me. He'd never hurt me." She withers into a ball, and curls like a sleeping kitten. "He loves me. He loves me."

"You just said he'd kill you or Makani. Does he love you, or love having you available for him?"

Maili bolts to her feet, pointing to the door. "Get out. Get out and never come back. I hate you."

Part of me wants to calm her, but the part that hates being yelled at wins out. I leave.

There's only one bicycle in the garage, a beater. Makani must still have his bike with him. Where would I go if I were Makani? I walk to the waterfront and think. People say a food truck in the parking lot has some great fish tacos. My turn in line comes and soon my hands are full, and my stomach jumps up and down with excitement. I sit at a picnic table to eat overlooking the ocean and the sea lovers in their suits, snorkel gear, and surfboards. The fish is local and fresh with lime and sauce. It tastes amazing.

Makani wouldn't try to pedal up to Waimea Canyon. It's too steep a climb. He doesn't have the skills Kekoa has to find local free food. He might have gone to one of his classmate's houses. Finding my way back to Maili's house, I climb the steps, open the screen, and knock.

Maili calls, "Go away!"

"It's me, Lily. Maili, I want to help you look for your son. Can I borrow your bicycle?"

She swears, and I hear her blow her nose. "Okay, go ahead. The password is Damianmylove."

I nod and shut the screen door. "Thanks."

The purple Omega bicycle is perfect for my height. I don't have to adjust the seat. The rest of the day, I bike through the residential areas of Poipu and Koloa, searching for Makani's bike in yards and on the shore.

By evening, I turn on the front and rear lights. I wonder if Makani ever returned to Poipu. If he lied to us about going home but stayed in Lihue, I should try that next.

Here I am, with no job, no place to stay, no friends other than Kekoa—who disappeared, and I'm hunting for someone else's child. But I have to locate him. A sinking feeling bounces around inside me. Makani's a poster child of someone who would take his life.

CHAPTER THIRTY-ONE

Kekoa

I go to bed at the shack hungry. Alone. Blown far from home. Even though I grew up just an hour's drive ride away, it might as well be across the ocean. My wrists are circles of wounds from the shackles on the ship and the rope when the demons threw me into the ocean. I try to set them down in a comfortable position, but I can't rest my arms in a position where they don't hurt. I rock in the hammock I made for Lily and think of her. As the light fades to gray, the room takes on a coldness, not in temperature, but aloneness. My room at home was about this size, but the shed only echoes my loneliness, silent and empty. At home, the day's memories of laughter, hugs, meaningful conversations with people who love me, learning, and, of course, great food, left me full at the end of the day.

I pray for my family, for Lily, my birthmother, and Makani—my poor brother.

The door creaks open. I lean forward. My heart has swung into action, catapulting through my veins while I listen. The room is dark. I roll off the hammock and leap on the man, pinning his arms behind his back the way my brothers and I used to.

A scream stops me dead in my tracks. "Lily?" I drop her arms.

She turns. "Kekoa." Her arms squeeze me. All that soft hair of hers covers my chest. Her hands stroke my bare shoulders.

I hold her as minutes amble by—like floating in the ocean on an inner-tube after the day's work is done. We sway back and forth, two magnets relishing every moment we're together. My hand holds her head against my heart while my other hand caresses her back. Neither of us wants to break the spell, but she pulls her head back and says, "I missed you so much."

Like easing into a hot tub, I breathe out my contentment. "I had this giant hole in me, thinking you went on the ship or flew home and left forever. Why didn't you go?"

"I can't leave you!" Her arms stroke my back.

She looks up at me with those beautiful, kind eyes, and she says, "I hope that doesn't scare you away."

My finger glides across her cheek. "I don't want to leave you either." My body wants to have married her yesterday. I pull her head to my chest because the intensity of her face being so close to mine is more than I can bear. Her soft hair slides through my fingers silkier than fur. "Okay, I'm banishing you to your hammock until morning."

"Tell me what happened to you." She pulls away and slides into her swinging bed.

We talk about our separate events.

"Makani never went home. He's missing. I rode all over Poipu and then biked to Lihue. My legs and arms are killing me."

I rub my neck when she tells me Makani is missing. My stomach sinks to my hips. "Oh no, I'm afraid he might kill himself."

"Exactly." Her voice carries a depth of concern. Empathy. "It's worse. Maili told the police she thinks you kidnapped him."

I shake my head. "The woman is delusional. Why would I kidnap my brother? That's a felony offense."

"I told her you wouldn't and hadn't. She didn't believe me."

I lean my head against the wall. "We have to find him."

Lily adjusts herself on the hammock. "The cops are searching for you."

Being a crook's scapegoat threatens my life. "We still have to find him. I'll talk to the pastor of my folk's old church. I hope he can loan us a car."

The next morning, we leave to borrow a car. Pastor Cason has a receding hairline, which makes me guess he's in his late forties, but his pool-blue eyes tell me he's at peace with himself and the world. His aloha shirt shakes from his laugh when he sees me. He's sitting at his desk, his bare feet sticking out from below, crossed. I see the pleasure emanating from his eyes as he stands and reaches his hand out for a shake. He must have known Dr. Lavada delivered live babies and had a hand in getting families. As if he's remembering laying me into Mom's waiting arms, he has no problem loaning us his beater Honda. If I wreck it, he'll just talk to Dad.

We cover the beaches on the Lihue side of the island first. Many people are living in their cars. Lily has never seen many of these beaches. If only we could visit them and linger in their majesty. I want us to hold each other's hands with our toes in the surf and take pictures of the palm trees and waves and the way the sun reflects on the water. We have to come again. For us.

Lily drives. I can duck down when we see any police, but none show themselves. We check out Lydgate Beach Park, moving up the coast on the east side of the island. A wedding reception fills the pavilion. The bride's joy emanates from her face and fills me with joy. Dad says few get married these days. Commitment means little. "Lily, why don't people get married anymore?" We walk down to the beach. Hundreds of people with colorful swimsuits, umbrellas, beach chairs, sand buckets and burned skin line the sand. Lydgate's rock wall enclosure lets only the tallest waves in. Inside the stone barrier, little fish can wash in. But after they grow, they can't get out. A dozen people's snorkels dot the surface of the water as they discover the bright-colored fish.

Lily takes her time to answer.

"I suspect most women want the man they choose to love them for a lifetime. It's hard for people to trust. It's hard for me to trust. Who comes from parents who were happily married? And then pornography and media train everybody to view women especially, like a piece of pie, to be eaten and judged, not to be known and cherished. Many people keep their options open but desire the benefits of marriage now."

"What about you? Do you want to be married in the future if you find the right guy?" Cold sweat beads on my face.

"I do want to be married someday and have children. What about you?"

"Yeah. But I have so much to learn about girls and relationships. I don't know how to go about creating a romance."

"Be my friend," she says. "Discover me as I discover you."

"Okay, friend." I bump shoulders with her. "I've been thinking about knowing versus being admired," I say.

"Yeah? How so?"

"Well, at home, we share everything. Mom makes us talk about what we're feeling. We all understand each other. But people on the ship crave the title—the toughest guy, the prettiest face or whatever. Marriage to me is analogous to the family I have at home. If you're not willing to share your feelings, it's like you never break your egg open and share it. If you can't mix with the flour, oil, milk, and leavening of other people's personalities, you can't be a pancake. Not until you learn to give yourself away. You can only be a big egg— a big, lonely egg."

"Give yourself away. I love that. And throw away your shell?" I hear her smile in the music of her voice.

"Yeah. Shell bits don't make good pancakes." I put my arm around her.

"Makani." Lily's focus turns to my brother. We search for the boy among hundreds of local kids with the same color of skin. The Lydgate beach stretches a half mile with heiau boulders placed by the ancient Hawaiians at the end of the parking lot.

I explain the stones. "These massive boulders symbolize mana, power, to the ancient Hawaiians. This area is protected by law." I don't see Makani, but a police car comes our way. The two officers look around. "Okay, incoming police. Let's go down to the beach."

We work our way down a slight incline to the water's edge to the north. The police car can't drive past the heiau. The road stops there. We circle up and hide behind some ironwood trees.

The police turn around and return to the pavilion. I hope they're not looking for me. If they are, it would be better to stay away from public areas, but we have to find Makani before he does something stupid.

We drive to Kapa'a.

"Lily, how can I disguise myself?"

She looks around, orienting herself. "Didn't we pass a thrift store by Cocoa Palms Hotel?"

I smile. "Yeah, I think we did."

Lily turns around.

At the thrift shop, we find a woman's long, white-haired wig, but Lily borrows a pair of scissors and cuts it short. I put it on along with a golf shirt and instantly become a grandpa.

"Okay, Gramps." Lily pulls my hand to leave.

The wig is hot. I'm not used to wearing a shirt, much less a knit one with a collar.

Lily laughs at me. We get into the car.

"Stick your stomach out if anyone sees you. You're too buff to be a grandpa."

I glance in the rear-view mirror. "So, this is what I'll look like in fifty years."

Lily turns the car around. "Plus a few dozen pounds, arthritis, high blood pressure, diabetes, wrinkles, sags, and bags under your eyes." She glances at me with a twinkle in her eyes.

"Not me. I'm keeping fit."

She stares at my chest. My reaction is to tense the muscles in my chest. How stupid is that?

"Speaking as an old woman of nineteen, it's not so easy to exercise when your knees hurt, and you're tired all the time. My mom is only fifty, but that's what she says. She looked similar to me at twenty, but gained a pound or two a year. Now she's fifty pounds overweight and feels ugly."

"Doesn't she swim?" I turn up the A/C.

"I competed in swimming in high school, but no, Mom doesn't swim. Ever."

We drive through Kapa'a looking for Makani, but don't see him or his bike. There's a strip of dirt by the narrow road where cars park. We find an empty spot. There's a paved twelve-mile walking and bike path that parallels the ocean. Lily rents bikes for two hours using cash.

There's a reef twenty yards out on the first beach, Baby Beach. The reef catches the surf, leaving an area for children to play in without the risk of oncoming waves. We don't see our boy anywhere. The clouds skip through the sky with the breeze. Lily's hair blows around, shining in the sun. The beauty of biking with Lily keeps pulling me out of the seriousness of our search. *Please God, help us find him. Help us help him.*

In North Kapa'a, we grab some Thai food and bottles of water from one of the food trucks and ride north. Kealia beach, the next beach, is busy with surfers, paddle boarders, and body boarders. I check the boy's bathroom and all around, but we don't find Makani. Some kids point at me and laugh. I'm not fooling anyone. Maybe from a distance, an officer might not check me out because I look too old. Proceeding, we stop for a breather and eat under an ironwood tree, hanging its long needles and cones down. The teal sea spreads out as the real feast in a sandy cove in front of us. Someone has built a driftwood hut and crafted the word "aloha" in the sand with driftwood.

"How much farther until the path ends?" Lily asks.

"A couple more miles."

Maili must be frantic. We reach the end and race our bikes back downhill to our car. It's dinner hour, so there are fewer people on the path. Once our bikes are dropped off, I walk to the car and see a policeman driving by. We flatten ourselves against the side of the building. By borrowing the car, there's no record of us using it. If we had rented one, I might have been marching off to jail right now. My heart slows to a horserace speed.

Lily giggles. "This might be fun if Makani's life wasn't in danger, or you weren't in danger of being arrested."

We both get dead serious. I peek around the corner. "Okay, let's go." We only have a couple of hours of sunlight left. Instead of hitting all the smaller beaches, we drive north. "Do you remember him saying anything about any place he might go?" I ask.

Lily bites her lip. "I'm thinking." She looks out the window, but I know she's praying.

I try to clear my mind and remember the words he said. "We're so helpless."

CHAPTER THIRTY-TWO

Kekoa

L ily pats my thigh as she drives north on the highway
in our search for Makani. "How would you kill
yourself? Maybe brothers think alike."

My foot jiggles. It seems to help me think. My shoulders
move up and down. The ocean isn't scary for me. I would
never try to die by drowning. It takes too long, and impulses
kick in to make you find air. "I'd jump off the Kalalau Trail
at sunset. You can't change your mind."

"Let's go." She picks up speed. It takes another hour to
arrive, past Hanalei Bay, over one-way bridges. We have to
drive slowly. Ke'e Beach is at the end of the road. The
highway that leads around the island stops there. No road is
possible. The Napali cliffs tower, dramatic, rugged, and
deadly. But we don't have a Hawaii driver's license or a

permit. You can't get into the park without those, and we only have an hour to find him if he's here.

Before we drive to the park station, we park in front of someone's house and sneak through the brush. Lily's sure we'll get lost. Our legs become scratched from blazing a trail in the jungle, and mosquitoes feast on us, but we have to go on. I long for my machete to whack this guinea grass and ferns out of our way. I pray we're not stung by any centipedes. We work our way downhill and end up on the road. The lifeguard tower sits in the center of the road facing the ocean. It's a small beach compared with Kealia, Kapa'a, and Poipu beaches. A cliff on the left marks the beginning of the incredible precipice that rises thousands of feet straight up.

"Hey, you guys aren't supposed to take the road. The boulders above the road come down. It's not safe," a lifeguard says to us. He's local, buff with black hair and a traditional teal swimsuit, instead of the lit ones most tourists wear.

"Thanks," I say. "And thank you for keeping people safe, Bro."

"Sure thing." He smiles and grabs a six-pack of water bottles from the cooler in the bed of the truck next to the tower.

I pull off my wig. "Hey, do you remember a kid who looks like me, alone, go by here and start up the trail?" I ask.

The guy looks at me, pauses, and says, "Matter of fact, I think so. A kid about fifteen?"

"Yeah, thanks. He was talking about suicide, and we're really worried about him."

The guard stops. "Oh no. Just a minute." He flies up the guard steps to the second level, where other guards are watching the beach, and comes down. After pulling the tailgate down on his truck, he digs through a big box and stands with a coiled nylon rope. "I'd like to help if I can."

I almost cry. "Whoa, I am so grateful."

"Hey, I'm Joshua," he says. "You must be his brother, since you two look alike."

"Yeah. This is Lily, and I'm Kekoa. But Makani and I didn't grow up together. I was adopted and just met him," I say.

Joshua is a father of a toddler, but the child lives with his mother. I can't imagine how hard it must be to have to visit your own child.

We clamber up the hill. Lily needs to stop and catch her breath, but I feel an urgency to keep going. Already the sun is making its royal exit, starting down with a golden scepter, casting a glow on the ocean and land. The trail is only eighteen inches wide in places, with dirt and rocks showing through the grass. There are no guardrails, and a rugged cliff jets down thousands of feet on my right. A guy with a walking stick and a woman want to pass us. I lean against the cliff to allow him room as they pass.

"It's amazing, and I wish we could stay longer. We have to return to L.A.," the young woman says. They rush to make it to the beach before sunset.

My side hurts, but we walk as fast as we dare. When we round a corner, the sun sprinkles the world with orange pixy dust. I hear up ahead, "Goodbye world"—Makani.

"Makani, wait for me, Brother. I love you." My feet fly up the trail. I stumble and clutch the crumbly rocks, and one leg goes over the rim. A tornado of energy flows out of my hands as I claw and pull with my arms, feeling for plants, a rock, anything to pull against. Panic pulses its poison through me. *God, help!*

Joshua comes up behind me and lies down. "I got you, Brother." He grabs my wrist and leans against the rock cliff in case he has to hold my weight.

I raise one leg up to the side of him, and he pulls it up. Jumping to my feet, we race to Makani.

"Slow down, Kekoa. You won't do your brother any good if you slip off before he can jump." Joshua's tone is calm but firm.

I hesitate. "Okay." *Lord, please, may he wait.* "Makani, I'm coming. Please wait for me."

Just as the sun dips, closing the day, flashing its green kiss as the sun passes through the water for the briefest of moments, I see Makani teetering on the rim. His hand is on the rocky cliff rising above him.

Joshua gives me the rope. "Secure him first. Talk later. We both take the rest of the rope, otherwise, he'll pull us both off the edge."

He's right. "Makani, thanks, Brother. I'd love to spend time with you. So many places I want to show you." I make a slip knot and swing it around his wrist. "This is because I love you. Please don't jump and take us both with you. Joshua has a baby girl who needs her daddy."

Makani sobs. "I want a daddy so much. Ever since I could talk, I'd beg Mommy to give me a daddy. But no." He swears and calls her words not worthy to echo down the mountain. "She told me I couldn't ever see you again."

"If you jump off the cliff, you will make Damian win," I say. "He was never father material. However, God has a father for you."

"Yeah, right? God? He made my life suck."

I take a deep breath and put my hand on Makani's shaking arm. "Come on; move toward me. I want to hug you and tell you some places I'll take you and things I'll teach you, just like my father taught me. He's old, but he's the best father anyone could ever have. And he will love being your father, too." I hold his hand. He stumbles, but I steady him. We move to a wider place, and I hug him. He shakes with convulsive sobs. I remember crying when I fell and ripped open my legs, diving into a mountain pool where we weren't supposed to dive. Dad just held me, too.

Joshua says, "It's dark. We've got to get down the trail. We'll rope ourselves together." He ties a rope around us and leads with Makani in the middle. We don't talk so we can concentrate on the trail. *Thank You, God.*

It takes hours to creep our way down, slipping but helping each other.

I don't see Lily until we arrive at the lifeguard station. She stands next to five police officers. "Kekoa, whatever your last name is because you're not in our records, you're under arrest for the murder of Ingrid Swenson."

"What?" Makani screams. "No." He turns to me and says, "Kekoa, did you kill someone?"

I shake my head.

CHAPTER THIRTY-THREE

Kekoa

I let the police put me in their car in handcuffs. Makani yells, "If you take him, I will really jump off the cliff next time. He's innocent." They forced the boy into the back seat of another police car.

I'm tempted to rant at the injustice, but I pray God will work it all out. Love will win. Mom said love is at the core of being social. "Love never fails."

It takes a couple of hours to drive to Lihue. I see Maili at the station. As soon as the officer lets me out, she sees the cuffs and starts screaming at me.

"He's all I have, and you tried to steal him from me." Venom radiates like a black sun from her. Poor Makani.

I say nothing. What can I say? She won't believe me. I'm in cuffs. Officer McKinley ushers me in and reads me my rights.

"You're allowed one phone call," the officer says and hands me a phone.

"I need a lawyer. Can I get one?"

He nods. "You can get a court-appointed lawyer. I'll see to it tomorrow. It's late, so we'll save our questions for the morning. The boy was returned to his mother; that's what matters most."

The guard makes me change my clothes into striped pants, a shirt, and rubber slippers before taking me to my cell. A light in the hall shines in my square eight-by-eight cell housing only a cot, a toilet, and a sink. I can read foul words etched onto the empty white walls by some device, perhaps a paperclip or the corner of a diamond ring. The room smells like bleach and mildew. It's odd, bleach kills mildew. Then I see the drain, and the mildew from the hole makes me sneeze. At least Makani is safe. Although, when I think about it, if he goes to his mother without my influence, he's destined to destroy his life—if Damian doesn't kill him first.

I pray for my family, those who want me, and those who don't. Love never fails. But I can't pray for Damian, except to ask that God change his heart. What kind of man cheats on his wife by keeping another woman—for eighteen years? What kind of man wants his son murdered so he can be rich?

In the morning, my leg muscles are stiff. Pus shows around the edges of the cut on my calf. A security guard shoves oatmeal mush through a compartment into my cell. I eat it with a paper spoon that weakens with each bite, and it does little to satisfy my hunger.

A team of two escorts me into a conference room of sorts. It's small with a stale tobacco smell to it. They question me about Ingrid. I tell them the entire story about Clint giving me the chip. God will be with me even if I join the military. I'm no longer afraid. If people laugh at me because of my ignorance, I'll live. It's their ignorance that shows, not mine.

Then Stuart McConnell, my lawyer, comes in. He's a portly, middle-aged man, in a hurry to talk and get it done. A game of golf awaits him when we finish.

"Kekoa, they have acquitted you of your kidnapping charge. Lifeguard Joshua Applebee said he came with you up the Kalalau trail and found Makani. That, in fact, you were heroic in saving the boy from jumping and risked your life to help him. Now, tell me all you know about Ingrid Swenson."

I revisit the complete story and then realize a blood test should clear me. "Please, have the police do a blood test on me and compare it to whatever DNA they have linking me to Ingrid's death. I'm not Clint. I took the chip because I was afraid, but I'm not Clint."

He sits back, stunned. "That's a wonderful solution." Shoving his papers and computer into his briefcase, he leaves.

I sit alone in the stuffy room. A nurse comes in and takes a vial of blood from my arm, a security guard by her shoulder. When I ask for a dressing for my leg, she says, "That's not my job. I do bloodwork."

A female officer returns me to my cell. She glances at my leg and says she'll send me to the nurse after lunch. But by the time I'd eaten my lentils and carrots, Officer Chin, a little woman with cropped black hair, comes and informs me I am being released. We walk down the hall as she talks. My DNA doesn't match that of Ingrid's killer. "We have a temporary wristcom you must wear, so whichever military branch wants you can contact you."

My head jerks forward. "How long do I have to get a birth certificate before the military takes me?"

She stops at the reception area and looks me over. I see the sadness in her eyes. "Technically, you already qualify for the military because you don't have a chip with your DNA recorded. If you can get it, you better get it ASAP." She takes off the shackles and straps a wristcom onto my red, sore wrist and sits at a desk in the office's corner. "I've programmed it on my computer so every arm of service can contact you.

With all the rioting in our beloved country, and the government seeming to race toward civil war, and the war in Thailand escalating, every branch of the military will want you. It'll just be a matter of who is fastest."

Rioting. Civil war. My knee jiggles like a dog shaking off swamp water. If only I could shake this edict so easily. "Can you give me a day?" Tears fill my eyes. I have to do more than just carry a gun for the rest of my brief life. I can see Mom and Dad's faces when they hear of my death. Their pain slams into my gut like a boulder after I've fallen from a rock face. "Please." My brothers. Is this their future, too? The injustice fills me with indignation, like adrenaline in a race. "It's not my fault I wasn't born. God made me live, not die." I stare into her to read her body language, mopping my tears, fearful of breathing lest I miss something.

Her head arcs back. She glances at the Sheriff's office door in the corner. Her jaw juts out on one side and then back.

Please, God. Please.

"Do you know your birthmother's identity?"

"Yes, Maili Lelani Kaaumoana." My voice croaks.

She glances at her computer, hits a few buttons, and says, "That is what your blood test DNA shows. But she won't grant permission for you to have a birth certificate?"

"Not so far. But I saved her son's life. Maybe now she'll let me live."

She mumbles, "Yeah, she's a piece of work." Then she jolts her face up. "You didn't hear me say that."

I nod.

"Okay, I'll give you a day before I turn on the device. But don't tell anyone I did this for you."

I nod and stand. "Can I keep the slippers?"

She smiles and stands too. "Sure, they're not my size." Her arms grab an electronic clipboard. "Here, sign under 'my signature' that I'm releasing you." She looks down and sees my infected leg. Her shoulders slump. "I can't let you go with that leg."

"I appreciate it, but I can't lose a minute. Maili has to accept me. She just has to." I sign, put on my own clothes, and leave.

Her lips twist in a frown. "Be here by eight in the morning with Maili, or I activate your wristband remotely. This mistake will be on my record, so make your life worth my mistake."

Why is giving people a chance to live a mistake? I push through the door. The clouds are dark, threatening a deluge. I have a day. One day.

CHAPTER THIRTY-FOUR

Kekoa

The time bomb is ticking. I sprint down the sidewalk toward the highway. Where can I go to catch a ride to Poipu from Lihue? A plane roars down to land at the airport across the street from me. If only I could ride with a tourist driving to his resort. At least the police aren't looking for me anymore, just Damian's killers. The verse keeps floating through my brain. "Everyone born of God overcomes the world" (1 John 5:4 NIV).

The sky is about to dump. I don't wait for the crosswalk, but sprint across the highway as soon as traffic allows. The busy airport spreads before me, including long TSA lines snaked around, packed with people waiting. People stand with suitcases talking on their phones or watching incoming traffic. I jog down the grassy incline and approach people.

"Are you traveling to Poipu?" I ask. At least I have on Makani's green t-shirt. I don't look as homeless as when I was bare-chested. A dozen people tell me no.

A middle-aged security guard approaches me in his navy uniform. "You can't bum a ride here. Leave now, or I'll call the police."

I return to the highway but see the adjoining street on my left, filled with rental car agencies and their clients, and jog over.

Reliable Car Rentals has many people waiting in line to get their vehicles, either cars or PlanePods. Standing in line, I listen to conversations. *Lord, please, I need a ride.* Only two people are behind the counter available to help customers.

A short, slender girl studies my leg. When I glance down, I see an oozing, bright red gash, and say to the girl, "I haven't had time to take care of it. It's a long story. I have to get to Poipu soon; my survival depends on it."

She whispers to her thin girlfriend with half-black, half-silver spikes of hair sticking out an inch in every direction. The shorter girl says, "We're driving to the Hyatt; you can hitch a ride with us."

"Thanks. You don't know how important this is to me."

The girl smiles. "Well, 'my life depends on it' sounds important."

I stand in the corner for twenty minutes by the clock on the countertop, but it feels like twenty hours.

The girls rent a red Mustang, and I help them load their suitcases.

The tall one says, "This is Jenna, and I'm Ashley. We're from Seattle."

"Aloha. I'm Kekoa, local."

Jenna says, "Gotta keep blood off the carpet. Sorry, this is gonna hurt." She dampens a tissue from a small box under the seat and fills it with hand sanitizer, then slathers it on my gash.

"Ow." My hand goes to my head. The pain is searing. "Thanks, I think."

She wipes the excess and the fluids pouring from my wound up with more tissue paper.

Ashley starts the car. I sit in the back seat and dab my wound, making sure it doesn't bleed.

It pours down rain outside. Traffic crawls, and it takes thirty minutes longer than normal.

They tell me about their lives in Seattle. I'm vague but tell them about our family's farmer's market and hunting pigs. They assume my wound is from our last pig hunt, and I let them think that. My legs bounce up and down from my nervous energy. To sit in a car with strangers, reminds me of walking into cobwebs at night. You don't know where the spiders are on your body. I don't know which girls are Ingrid spiders and which are gold treasures.

As soon as we arrive in Poipu, I get out and thank the girls. My leg is stiff and hurts when I put pressure on it. I limp the two miles to Maili's house in Poipu as water and pus ooze down my leg, a sitting duck for Damian's gang. The street is empty, no thugs in sight. I knock on the screen door, since the wood one is open. Maili talks to a friend in a normal tone of voice. The Maili I haven't met. She comes to the door.

"Jen, I'll get back to you. There's someone at the door." She throws the phone on the sofa and opens the door. "Kekoa."

I hear the stiffness in her voice—the guilt. She knows she's misjudged me now. I walk into the entry and living room. The air is thick.

"Is Makani okay?" I ask.

"Yeah, he's fine. He's at school." She sits on the couch, and I ease into a padded chair across the room.

I wait.

"Listen, I. . ." She rubs her hands together and peers out the window. "Do you want anything to drink?" Rising, she opens the refrigerator and pulls out a tropical drink, opens it, and pours it into a pretty glass with a teal starfish on it—all blown glass.

"No thanks." I'm too nervous to drink, and I'd probably spill it.

She sits again and takes a sip. "I need to apologize. Makani told me he went to the Kalalau trail to jump off, and you talked him down. Thank you. That boy means the world to me." She looks at me as if she swallowed a mynah bird.

"He means a lot to me, too. My brothers, the ones I grew up with, are so special to me. I adore them, and I love Makani too. You can trust me to be a brother to Makani. He needs me. Really, really needs me."

She sniffs. "I know, now." Her eyes look flat somehow. "But the thing is, Damian is still after you." Maili shakes her head. "He won't give up until you're dead." She looks down. "The more Makani gets attached to you, the more it will hurt when he finds out."

"When he finds out his father killed me?"

Maili's head twists, and she swallows. "It is what it is."

"Okay, I can see you can't stand up to Damian. Will you help me? Take me to the Lihue police station and sign a paper saying you authorize me to get a birth certificate?"

She looks like I've thrown ice water on her face. "No, I mean, Damian would be mad at me. If I permitted you a birth certificate, I'd acknowledge that I let you be born, that I want you to live." Her hand goes to her lips. "I wanted you with all my heart. I cried and begged Damian to let me keep you." She looks out the window as if his words are echoing off it. "He said there would be a time when we could have our own babies. He'd divorce his wife and marry me."

How do I say this? "When you're sixty and after his father-in-law dies, and he inherits millions, perhaps then he'll marry you, but I doubt it. Can't you see that his promises are all a fantasy he uses to control you? Otherwise, even if he doesn't love his wife, how can he do that to his kids—the ones he raised?" A cold wall erects between us. "The truth is, he's a killer. He uses you, knowing you have something he wants.

Just as God made me in your womb, He made you and loves you. Find someone who will love you and show it by his actions, not just his words.

Her eyes narrow, but she isn't screaming like before.

I continue, "Let love win. Love for Makani, love for me, love for you. You don't need Damian."

"Oh, I do, I need Damian. He's the love of my life." She puts her hands around her arms like a self-hug.

"He's not the love of anything; Damian has a wife he hasn't divorced."

Maili says, "That's ..." and then stops.

This may be my only chance; I say, "Please, take me to the police. Sign papers for a birth certificate. God will deal with Damian. Let love, genuine love, win in your life."

She sits staring at her hands, and a tear falls down her cheek, then several.

I bring her the tissue box from across the room.

"I didn't want it to be this way."

Sitting next to her, I put my hand on her arm.

"I couldn't leave him." Her sobs contort her voice. "He told me I was nothing without him, and I believed him."

"But that's not true. If you are weak, let God be strong through you. Let God take care of Damian and take care of you."

"I can't." Her voice whines with hopelessness, and she clings to me.

My arms pull her into a hug. "You mean, you haven't yet. But you can. You can find a job and develop your skills without Damian. You've been a property manager, and Poipu has other owners who can use your skills." I stroke her back.

She calms and rests her head on my shoulder.

I pray silently for her and Damian, both caught in their lies. "Maili, Mom, what's the lie that Makani believes that drove him to want to kill himself?"

She sits up, looking puzzled, and her mouth opens and closes. "I suppose he thought I don't love him, but I do."

"Could it be that you believe the lie that Damian loves you when he doesn't?"

Maili sinks into the couch, her head tips back. "I've known it for a long time. It's just so painful to accept."

"Makani needs you to be you, not an extension of Damian. Let God fill you with real love, genuine peace, and eternal hope. Switch to Him. The woman God made you to be is still forming in you. Feed on God's love; it's real."

"I don't know how," she says.

"God does it in you if you surrender to Him, and I can help you. We can find a sound church, and a women's group, for love and support."

"Maybe I did something right by conceiving you." Her eyes are tender.

A lump sticks in my throat. She wanted me dead, and now she's proud of me.

She looks at me like I'm a new person. Her hand strokes my hair. "You're beautiful— the best of Damian and me."

Excitement ziplines through my veins, and I take a deep breath. "Mom, will you give me a birth certificate? It's not too late to give me a future."

She shrinks down. "But Damian, he's going to kill you."

An idea comes to me. I've had to forgive my mom in order to bring me to this moment, and perhaps God will grant me the same if I forgive my enemy—my birth father. *Okay, God, take my bitterness and hatred of Damian for what he's done to Maili, me, and Makani. I forgive you, Damian. Regardless of whether I feel like it. God, take me the rest of the way.*

"Can I use your phone?" I ask.

"Who are you calling?" Her voice trembles.

"Damian, please dial it for me." I hold my hand out.

She turns white. Her hand shakes as she finger-identifies on her hand-held cell phone and then hands it to me. I look at her contact list and push the button for Damian.

CHAPTER THIRTY-FIVE

Kekoa

I dial Damian's phone, and it rings.

He says, "Not now. Call me later." The timbre of his voice sounds like mine but impatient, and in charge.

"Damian, this is Kekoa." The phone goes silent.

"Who?"

"Kekoa, your son." *God, keep my voice from shaking.*

"I don't want to talk to you. You don't exist," he says.

"I exist. To kill me won't keep your wife or your father-in-law from finding out the truth. We're past that now; the police have proof. I can send our pictures, Makani, your second son, and mine, to your wife and in-laws. Not for money. I just want you to stop trying to kill me."

"I'm not trying to kill…" He fake coughs. "Look, I can't talk right now. What do you mean, my second son? Oh, never mind. Goodbye."

"Damian. Now. Call off your goonies. I'm not just thinking about Maili and her suffering for having to give up or hide her children. I'm considering your wife. I don't want this to destroy your family. You should be faithful to your wife and restore your marriage. You want your kids to respect you."

He waits and clears his throat. "Give me a minute," he says to someone by him. "Okay, what are you going to do?" He's speaking to me now.

"Nothing, I don't want revenge. I just want to live and have those around me, including you have a chance at happiness. But you can't be happy holding this deception. Since you've cheated on your wife all these years and kept secrets, you have no basis to trust her because she might have secrets too. You can't understand trust when you're not trustworthy. The police have my blood and verified that I'm your son. If I die, you'll be the first person they'll suspect, and any harm to me will make you look bad. A good reputation, trust, and respect—all that will be gone. Your kids and wife will know, your business associates, and your father-in-law."

The phone is silent. "Okay, I'll do what you're asking and talk to you later."

"Okay, bye." The phone goes dead.

Maili looks at me as if I had just transformed from a chrysalis into a butterfly in front of her. She blinks away tears. "It's done," she says and sits. Her hands press between her knees, as her glazed eyes stare out the window.

"It's done." I pray it's done, and that Damian meant it when he agreed to let me live. I won't know until I live or die, I say.

After sitting for a few minutes readjusting to the dissolving lie she's believed all this time, she stands. "Can I get you a sandwich?"

I realize how hungry I am. "Yes, I'm starving." I stand. "Can I help?"

She turns to answer me and notices that I'm limping. "What happened?"

I show her my gash. "I fell off the Kalalau Trail and cut my leg. Joshua, a lifeguard, came with us and pulled me back up."

"Oh, no." She leans to examine my leg and disappears into the bathroom.

"Hold still," she says and dresses my wound. A smile covers my face. My mother is taking care of me.

After I down three sandwiches, we drive to Lihue to sign my birth certificate. While I sit next to Maili in her white Tesla coming back, I chat about our canyon, my parents, and my brothers. It seems like a fairy tale to her. Her family has never approved of Damian. She's been rejected all these years. I can't wait to meet her family—my family.

My heart races as we drive back from the police department with all my new possibilities now that I have a chip in my hand, my chip. I can go to a community college here in Kauai. To imagine sitting next to girls in college doesn't hold the same appeal as it once did. It's Lily I want by my side. I can get a driver's license, buy, and keep the money I earn. Mom and Dad aren't at risk anymore since I have a birth certificate.

Maili chats about growing up in Waimea. Her extended family all lived together in a big old shack. No one could afford to get their own housing. She slept on a blanket behind the couch. Her brother slept on the couch. She met Damian when she worked at the Sheraton resort cleaning rooms. He came in and saw her, asked her for dinner, and then seduced her. He was in his mid-twenties and had just married his wife. Twice a year, he'd come to Kauai, sometimes with his spouse. Then he'd sneak off to Maili in the middle of the night or while his wife believed he was golfing. He trained her to be his property manager.

"God loves you and proved it with actions. He sent His Son to die for you. What an opposite, huh? Switching from the man who tried to kill your son, to the God who let His Son die for you."

Her eyebrows curve down a bit like she is trying to fathom the old fairy tale about God being true.

We're nearing her house, and I say, "Can we talk about it again?"

She says, "Yes, I'm going to need all the help I can get."

Lily sits on the lanai steps, sees me, lights up, and starts running toward me.

Once I'm out of the door, I fly toward her, pick her up by her waist, and swing her around. Her face glows like a torch on the blackest night. I put her down, and we wrap each other in a tight hug. We sway back and forth.

She laughs. "Kekoa, Kekoa, Kekoa, I keep losing you."

"Never again," I say. "Maili gave me a birth certificate. See?" I show Lily my slit wrist, the bandage over the chip and skin.

"What?" She looks at Maili. Mom has tears coming down her face, tears of joy.

I put out my arm for Mom and the three of us hug when Makani's yellow bus stops. With a hiss, the door opens.

"I want in." He drops his backpack on the ground and runs to us, and we all hug.

His classmates whoop out their windows as we drive off. I can almost hear the angels joining them.

Maili invites us to spend the night. I sleep in Makani's room and Lily sleeps on the couch. We make plans. Maili will search for a property management job. I'll get a job in a restaurant as a server and pay to stay with her on a trial basis and enroll in college. Lily wants to stay on Kauai too. She'll try to find a Christian family who will let her rent a room and go to Kauai Community College as well.

The next morning is Saturday. I wake up at 4 a.m. as if I'm going pig hunting. Dad and my brothers will eat breakfast soon. After pulling on my clothes, I go for a walk in the dark to thank God and wrap my brain around my mother's change of heart. A soft breeze blows, but I don't need a jacket. The sky's darkness wraps the world in mystery. I head toward the beach.

An uncanny sense of being watched makes me uncomfortable. A scurry behind me alerts me, and I turn around. A club to my head sends me to the ground. I start to get up, but a man, short and stocky, wrestles me to the ground, stronger than anyone I've known. He pins my hands behind me. After a moment, I realize it's Silver. His breath smells like beer.

"You're too late, Silver," I say.

"Silver is never too late."

His lightning eyes are inches from me. He pulls one of my hands and yanks me onto my stomach.

"I already gave the police the information about Ingrid. They took my blood sample to prove I didn't kill Ingrid," I say.

"Well, that's inconvenient." He twists my arm behind my back.

Sharp dagger-like pains in my shoulder immobilize me. "I'm of no benefit to you now," I say.

He laughs. "Your sorry carcass is going to make me rich." He swears. "I even quit my job because after I show Damian a picture of your dead body, I'm a rich man."

"No." I squirm. "I talked to Damian yesterday. He's telling his wife the truth about Maili. You can't blackmail him anymore." A gun cocks.

"You're lying," he says.

"Call him. Ask him. If you kill me, the police will just give you another murder charge. Damian will testify against you."

Shot after shot fires. He releases my arms. More shots. I don't know whether I've been hit. I can't move or think. An avalanche of murder surrounds me. More shots. Puffs of grass fly around me. My ears ring. Time disappears. I can't believe what I'm hearing. My life is over. Lily. Mom. Makani. My brothers and parents. I hear sirens.

He swears.

Sirens—closer.

I roll over on the grass in time to see him put the gun to his temple.

"No one gets Silver." His nose rises in the air when he stands like the victor. He pulls the trigger. The sound echoes off the houses.

"Noooo!" I bolt to my feet as his eyes roll back, and his body careens to the ground, pouring blood from both sides of his head. My feet back up a few steps. I feel myself and look at my body. No bullet holes. He just wanted to scare me. I can't stop shaking but collapse to the ground and hug my knees.

Police cars blare up to us. Three officers jump out of the car and hold a gun on me as they approach.

"He shot himself." My voice sounds woody and wobbly.

They take me to the police station—again. Once I am cleared and can leave, it's three o'clock. I walk most of the way to the farmer's market on the other side of Lihue still hearing shots in my head. It's over, God, I give you the terror of having someone shoot at me. Peace fills me.

I see Mom and Dad set up. My brothers are unpacking and bringing boxes from the van. I run. "Mom, Dad." My legs are rubber. I'm in their arms, and we all cry. I hug Mom, and Dad joins. Canyon pushes his way in, and then Kana. Auntie puts her arms around the lot of us. We have so much to talk about, and so much to be grateful for.

~ ~ ~

I'm in the van with my folks, brothers, and Lily, heading home. Makani and Maili will have to wait to see the canyon when the vehicle isn't already so full. Lily, holding my hand, sees Canyon's bronzy-golden hair and his atlas body, but her eyes keep drifting to me.

OTHER BOOKS IN

THE NEVER TRIO SERIES

Coming:

THE NEVERKNOWN

&

THE NEVERSEEN

If The Neverborn has touched you, **please** give back, rate it on Amazon, drop a comment, and share it. Kekoa and I need your support. Thank you!

Sign up to receive notifications when new books come out at <u>www.authorbbbrighton.com</u>

to receive a **free copy** of the Never Trio Prequel:

THE RITE OF PASSAGE